A COUNTRY FOR DYING

A COUNTRY FOR DYING

a novel

ABDELLAH TAÏA

translated by Emma Ramadan

SEVEN STORIES PRESS
NEW YORK • OAKLAND • LIVERPOOL

This work received support from the French Ministry of Foreign Affairs and
the Cultural Services of the French Embassy in the United States through
their publishing assistance program.

Seven Stories Press
140 Watts Street
New York, NY 10013
www.sevenstories.com

Library of Congress Cataloging-in-Publication Data

Names: Taïa, Abdellah, 1973- author. | Ramadan, Emma, translator.
Title: A country for dying / Abdellah Taia ; translated from the French by
    Emma Ramadan.
Other titles: Pays pour mourir. English
Description: First edition. | New York : Seven Stories Press, 2020.
Identifiers: LCCN 2019027770 | ISBN 9781609809904 (paperback) | ISBN
    9781609809911 (ebk)
Classification: LCC PQ3989.2.T27 P3913 2020 | DDC 843/.914--dc23
LC record available at https://lccn.loc.gov/2019027770

Printed in the USA.

9 8 7 6 5 4 3 2 1

For my sisters, all my sisters

PART I
Paris, June 2010

1. Apart

HE DIED YOUNG.

Fifty-six years old, that's young. Right?

It's the average age in Morocco, I know. The life expectancy. That's what they call it.

But he, my little father, gentle and furious, he didn't have time for anything. Not to live well, not to die well. It happened quickly. Barely two years.

One day, he fell. A collapse. A faint. Tremors. What's happening in his body?

We brought him to the public hospital in Rabat. He stayed there for four months. And then we brought him back to his house. Our house. Our little place. Our can of sardines with red chilies. A first floor that was relatively clean thanks to our mother, who was both messy and super manic. And a second floor that was well constructed but still unfinished. Rooms without doors, without paint. A cement-colored decor for a life to come, a future to build once money started falling from a permanently bright blue sky.

That's where we put him, our father, where we slowly forgot him, ignored him.

It was my mother, of course, who made all the decisions. She'll never admit it.

The doctors said that she had to protect the children, distance them from possible contagion. Separate them from the father's sick body.

It was because they didn't know what was going on, those heartless quacks. The order had to be executed, end of story.

My mother doesn't want to talk about it anymore. What happened in the past is in the past. Those are her words, about her own past. Not ours. Not mine.

I said nothing. The idea of protesting didn't even cross my mind. I saw everything, followed everything. A living father, still young, whom they decided to exile in his own house one day, and I keep on breathing, sleeping, dreaming each night of Allal and his big cock, imagining it in great detail. Just above the room where I slept, amidst the bodies of my many sisters who hadn't yet married, there was my father. Alone. A room that was too big, with no bed. Three Le Tigre blankets, placed on top of each other, served as his living space, where he could continue to be sick. Hope for recovery. The final rest.

Why didn't I say anything? Why was I so indifferent, so callous?

I didn't think my father was going to die. But I accepted, just like everyone else, that I wouldn't see him again.

That defeated father with his vanishing virility, I too participated in his murder. And yet no one brought charges against me. Not yesterday, not today.

I am free. In Paris and free.

No one can force me back into my former state as a submissive woman. I am far from them. Far from Morocco. And I'm talking to myself. I search for my father in my memories.

The weight of his heavy footsteps echoes in my ears.

I would listen to my frantic heart. I would try to calm it, soothe it so that it would stop pounding like a volcano in my chest. I would speak to it without opening my mouth. I would sing to it in Arabic and, sometimes, in French. Nothing helped. At night the heart revolts, it relives the day and its events without us, without our permission. Without me. More than a panic, it was a catastrophe, for I knew that if it stopped, I would die.

I didn't want to die. I couldn't sleep. Drift off. Give in to slumber. I resisted in fear.

My father's footsteps, separated from us, on the second floor, in a different darkness, sometimes saved me. My father didn't walk. He struck the ground. His heels went *boom-boom, boom-boom. Boom-boom.* Below, on our side, his reverberating footsteps made everything vibrate: furniture, windows, tables, television.

My father, no doubt also incapable of falling asleep, would wander around the unfinished second floor.

His footsteps communicated something else, too. Anger? Yes, of course. Fear? Perhaps. Dry tears? Certainly, but no one saw them.

A circus lion suddenly old, in a cage suspended in midair. Within his body, his breath fizzles out, little by little, night after night, one footstep followed by another.

I find them again, those footsteps. I listen to them.

My father paces in the back room. He crosses the patio. He turns around. He goes in circles. He touches the walls. He looks at the sky above the sinister ceiling. He goes far, all the way to the other room, the one off the street. I don't hear him anymore. No one hears him.

Sleep approaches. It will deliver me. Communion, at last. I leave. I travel. I forget my father. I don't even tell him goodbye.

But that man, familiar and foreign, I see him open his mouth, he's going to say something, a word, a name, a first name. One time. Two times. Three times.

Zahira. Zahira. Zahira.

Why me?

From Paris, years later, I answer him.

What do you want, my papa? What do you need? Are you hurting? Hurting terribly? Where? Where? Speak. Tell me, now. I'm all grown up now. I can handle things, even incomprehensible things. Show me where you hurt. Your stomach? Where in your stomach? Your guts? Your guts again? Those horrible spasms you inherited from your own father? Is that it?

Take my hand. I'm coming to the second floor. Here it is, my right hand. Guide it. It will see better than me what torments you, breaks you into pieces, makes you lose your mind, your way, your breath. Take it, take it. It's yours and it comes from you, this hand. Hold it. Caress it. Do with it what you like, whatever your heart and skin tells you.

Speak, if that's what you want. Die. Come back to life. Wander with me, with my hand, my unconscious. Stride across this second floor like a blind man, a desperate man, the madman you are despite yourself. Go. Go. Don't hold back. Love doesn't end. I'm not the one who says so. I'm not the one who knows so. Somewhere, in my shadowy body, lives make decisions for me and for you.

Think of your sister Zineb. When you were little, you adored her. You were still living at the foot of the Atlas Mountains when she disappeared. She was your second mother, wasn't she? Your sweetheart. Your only sweetheart. One night, she left with your father to look for a mysterious treasure hidden in a distant forest. One week later, your father came back without her. He never wanted to say what happened. From one day to the next, Zineb was lost forever. You would never see her again. Was she kidnapped? Sold to some rich lord in the countryside? She wasn't dead. She wasn't dead. That's what you told yourself in order not to lose all hope. That's what you still tell yourself today. Think of her, Papa. Think hard. Zineb. Zineb. Zineb. I think of her, too. I whisper her name. I envy her even. Her destiny must have been free. I don't see it like that. And you, my papa? How do you imagine Zineb's life? Long, happy, fulfilled? You want to join her, find her there, wherever she is now? Is that it? Am I wrong? Do I understand nothing of Zineb and her disappearance?

I was naïve. I am unhappy. And alone. So alone in Paris. In the center and yet as though at the edge of the world.

I hear your footsteps, my father. They come back. They exist. You walk. You go back and forth. You count, you play, you trace regions, countries, dark zones where we can see everything.

You are sick up there.

We are below, almost underground.

In our home, no one has changed, moved. We look at each other as before. We brush past each other. We are sick of being together. We have to leave, it's urgent. But we have nowhere to go to dream up something different. So: We blind ourselves. We don't sing anymore. We eat, we piss, we shit, we sleep. No one enjoys themselves anymore. Especially not our mother.

Your sister Daouiya doesn't visit anymore. Your older brother keeps her from leaving the house. She tells him that she misses you. He replies that sooner or later she will see you again. But not here. Not on this earth. Not in this world. Not for as long as she lives.

Within you, my father, there is fear. I imagined it frigid. I was wrong. That fear kept you moving. Death spread rapidly through your body, but it wasn't death that made you tremble.

Even after, in the tomb, in the sky, there is nothing. There will be nothing.

That's what you used to say sometimes, on certain dark days. Isn't that right?

You would get up. You would walk. Again. Again. And every night, on that unfinished second floor, that certitude became an absolute truth, indisputable.

The setting of your final months, you wanted to breathe

it in inch by inch. Leave a little breath there. A secret. Better than a memory. A cry.

My papa, to somewhat reassure you in your tomb, I want to believe that there is something else. Like you, I didn't believe anymore. I am changing my mind, here, now. Life doesn't end. Death cannot exist everywhere. The body doesn't end. It speaks with another tongue. It reinvents itself, endlessly. Up above, it transforms.

Today, my hand says this to you. Listen to it. Entrust it with a message, a role, a glance for me. And walk. Walk. Walk, on your second floor. You don't disturb me anymore. I have become what I am. It's my nature. A prostitute. They come to quench their thirst with me, in me. Everyone. Men and, sometimes, women. I no longer resist this destiny. The time for struggle is over.

You smoked all my life, my father. Except the last two years. You enveloped us in smoke at the house each day. No one ever complained.

There are people who smoke with arrogance, distance, selfishness. Not you. Not with your cheap cigarettes. I have the taste of them in me, in my nostrils, my tongue, my throat. You smoked three brands. Poor-people brands, of course. You started with Dakhlas. Ten years. Before I was born. In the mid-eighties, you switched to Favorites. And in 1990, just after the month of Ramadan that caused you so much suffering and that you didn't care for, you switched to Casas. From Casablanca. You had no love for that city, too noisy, too busy. But you adored its cigarettes.

You fell ill in a strange way. I didn't see it happen, but the image of that moment was evoked so many times in our home. Our mother recounted each detail of your decline to serve as a warning to us.

"Don't smoke! Don't smoke! Always remember what happened to him, his terrible illness!"

I'm forty years old. I've never smoked. I followed her advice. Her story.

You were still living among us, on the first floor. One Thursday morning, you didn't want to go to the hammam. Probably because you were sick of seeing the neighbors there, always nasty, jealous, and mean. You walked towards the patio and you yelled:

"Run me some hot water!"

It wasn't a yell as in former days. Your voice suddenly needed to exert a superhuman effort to give an order and at the same time hide your weakness. It betrayed you. It displayed the final traces of a virility that was already disappearing, for all of us to see. Did you know?

Then, in a vague way, I understood that something bad was happening to you.

My papa will collapse. I have to do something to stop it.

I was alone in our bedroom. I replied with a weak word, monotone, emotionless:

"Okay!"

When the water in the large boiler was hot enough, I put it in the room with the toilet. We didn't have a shower or bathtub. The Turkish toilet was where we washed ourselves when we were in a state of impurity and urgently needed to purify ourselves.

Were you in a state of impurity, or were you just dirty?

I didn't ask myself the question that day.

When did you step into the Turkish toilet?

Like a cat in the middle of the night, you crossed the patio sneakily and sought out privacy in that narrow space.

I suddenly heard your zipper and belt unfastening. Your pants fell.

You carried out the rest in silence. You turned on the tap. You approached the boiler. You cooled down the hot water a bit. Then you poured everything into the little red tub.

With your hands clasped, you started to splash yourself. I hear that water, its path: from your hands it moves towards your body, your torso, your chest, your neck, your chin. The rest of your face.

The hot water, delicious, arrives, it strikes you. You say: "Allaaaaahhhh!"

I smile.

You begin again.

The water. Your body. Your nudity. Your cries of pleasure.

"Allaaaahhh!"

Again and again.

You are well, very well. You are no longer weak and you never will be again. That brief moment with the hot water convinces you that solitude can be joyous. You are a child. You play. You forget yourself. You forget that we can hear you, can follow from a distance and imagine in detail what you are doing.

I'm supposed to be peeling the vegetables. I've stopped. I'm listening to you.

"Allaaaahhh! Allaaaahhh! Allaaaahhh!"

You weren't ashamed to express your joy. I wasn't ashamed to spy on you.

Two yards separated the children's room, where I was, from the bathroom. Your pleasure made the distance disappear. I was with you.

But I left too early. Someone knocked on the door.

And I didn't save you.

My mother told us what came next. You had told her, a week later.

This is what she said. It's all in my ears. It's short, and precise. Very precise.

"After washing up, he wanted to do his ablutions, as is customary. He realized he didn't have much hot water left. He stared at the bottom of the red tub. Five seconds. He decides that it should be enough. He will be very careful.

"He begins the ablutions. His private parts. In front. Behind. The mouth three times. The nose three times. The face three times. Each arm three times. Each foot, too. Then the ears. The scalp.

"He's succeeded. He's relieved.

"He gets up. He notices he still has soap under his armpits. But there's no more hot water. So he rinses them with cold water from the tap. Big mistake, and immediately he feels the consequences. He says to himself: My body was in summer and now it's in winter. I will surely fall ill. He guessed right. He thought he would catch a cold. He caught worse than that.

"It's his own fault. He smoked almost all his life. Cold and hot mixed together so closely in a fragile chest, riddled

with holes, like his, as if he wanted . . . As if he wanted . . .
to . . . to . . . As if everything was decided that day, in that
moment . . ."

Our mother didn't dare pronounce the word. It scared
her. It scared us, too.

Suicide.

She finished her story each time with these words:

"So now you've been warned. Pay attention when you
wash your armpits. Cold and hot together, or one after the
other, under your armpits—never! Understand? Never!"

How could that woman, that mother, forget that she wasn't
talking about a stranger, a neighbor, an enemy, but about
her husband, our father? His body is our body. Even ill, he
is ours, of us.

Why protect us from him? What he has, what he will
have, we will end up catching it, too. What's the point of
keeping our distance from him? What's the use of such
pitiful warnings?

"Stay away, stay away . . ."

Very soon after, they brought you to the big hospital in the
capital, Rabat.

I was in high school. I didn't come home for lunch. A
man who had been hanging around me for some time had
managed to lure me to his apartment. He entered me. And
he said: "I see that I'm not the first. I'm disappointed. Very
disappointed." He wasn't kidding. Afterwards, he tossed
me fifty dirhams. "So you can buy yourself something. Lipstick, for example." He wasn't kidding then, either.

That night, as soon as I stepped foot in our house, I felt that something was different.

"They took him to . . ."

I went to the bathroom. I took a deep breath. Papa is still here. You are here . . . You are here . . .

With my school uniform still on, I went out for a walk. My footsteps led me to the soccer field, deserted. The fifty dirhams were in the left pocket of my pants. Three bills: two twenties and a ten. I tore them up into a thousand pieces. I crouched down. I dug a small hole. I buried the pieces inside.

No trace. Day of mourning in advance. Day of ending. Of everything. Absolutely everything.

How to live after that, after that departure?

A house without a father. Only the mother: radiant dictatress, on her throne.

Cry? No. Tears are useless. Go back home? Yes, but only physically.

Can you hear me, Papa? I am finally grasping the meaning of what I lived, of what I lost.

I didn't rebel.

I never again saw the man who gave me the fifty dirhams.

But I went to visit Sawssane the Irish girl. My only friend. She lived in the old town of Salé, and it was with her that I learned, little by little, to protect myself from men while making them pay.

I didn't tell her what happened at our house, what was happening in me. But as soon as she saw me she could tell how much I was suffering.

She brought me to the hairdresser and asked them to dye my hair blond. I didn't protest.

My face, with that new color, transformed. My eyes became bigger. My nose smaller. My cheeks hollowed. And all around my head, fire.

The hairdresser turned me into what he wanted. He massaged me, for a long time. He touched me, softly, differently. He caressed my neck, my scalp, my forehead, my cheeks.

He didn't want to do me harm. His hands moved back and forth around my head. Played with my hair. Pulled my hair, hard, very hard. I liked that: a little violence.

The hairdresser's hands were like yours, Papa. Exactly the same. Large. Never-ending. Hands for another body, another world.

I closed my eyes. The whole time.

My friend Sawssane wasn't far. She devoured all the issues of the magazine *Al-Mawed* that were in the salon. She sang. English words. Sad and soft. Soothing through their repetition. I didn't understand the words. I recognized them. It was an ABBA song.

Sawssane comes from far away. She has freckles all over her body. Her hair is red. It smells good. She really does come from far away, very, very far away.

In the eighteenth century, the pirates of our town, Salé, attacked the ships of Christians, nonbelievers, Europeans, who passed near Morocco. They stole the riches being transported and sank the ships. They say that they brought Christian women back to Salé, kidnapped them, again and again. Irish women. They converted them to Islam, by force. The women quickly became Arabs, Muslims. And on top of it: women of Salé. Better guardians than anyone else of that corsair memory, those women who were slightly mad, slightly combative, always uncontrollable.

She is here in front of me. Sawssane, woman from the past, from another time. Gentle. Tender. Machiavellian. She taught me everything. Love, sex, secrets. I owe her everything. I am not angry at her.

Later, the world would end up turning that Irish girl into something other than what was planned. From one day to the next she would abandon her job as a madam. She would go to Mecca to repent and become pure once again.

Mother of a family, Sawssane! I never would have thought!

I'm told she has three girls now, with red hair like her, as pale and foreign as she is.

Sawssane calls me sometimes. I send her money. Not much.

Sawssane knows that you're gone, Papa. Every time we talk on the phone, though, she asks me the same question: "How's your father?" And at the end, she always asks me to tell you hello.

She prayed for you at Mecca. She said your last name and your first name aloud. Does that make you happy, up there?

Do you hear all the prayers I say each day for you?

Do you still remember François Mitterrand, the president of France? Over there, where you are, from one sky to another, have you met him? Has his appearance changed, his personality? Does being in heaven suit him? Does death soothe him?

It was winter. The moment of your final departure was drawing near.

Autumn had spared you, but as soon as the cold settled in for good in Salé, you stopped walking. You no longer turned in circles on the second floor. You almost never got up to stretch your legs, to give the illusion that you were still resisting. You remained splayed out. Day and night, night and day. You didn't even watch television anymore. The small screen of your TV set demanded too much concentration. Your eyes could no longer focus. You saw double. And that heightened the fatigue, the confusion, the questions that were too deep and had no answers.

What were you doing then? Tell me, little Papa, tell me . . .

"I was dreaming . . . I was preparing myself . . . I was already no longer there, in that life."

"That I know, Papa . . . But what else?"

"I learned to stop breathing. To do without the air here, in this world where you still live. I took my own breath away. And I observed what was happening."

"What? What, Papa?"

"I was rising up. I was no longer sick. My lungs, which had betrayed me, were renewing, regenerating."

"You were being reborn?"

"No."

"I don't understand, Papa . . ."

"I didn't want to stay alive, deprived of taste, salt, blood, sugar."

"Mama stopped going up to see you at night, I know. I know."

"She killed me."

"Don't say that, Papa."

"She killed me. Don't protect her."

"Yes, Papa. But sometimes, I understand her side, too. The world asked too much of her. She was the one who had to manage everything, steer everything, organize everything."

"She killed me, I'm telling you. Killed, ruthlessly. Don't anger me, Zahira."

"Okay, Papa. Okay, little Papa. Let's talk about something else. Let's talk about François Mitterrand. Why did you love him?"

"I didn't love him."

"Are you sure you didn't love him?"

"I'm more than sure."

"Then why did you come down to our home, below, to look at the last images of his life, his visit to Egypt, his funeral?"

"I wanted to catch his death."

"'Catch his death,' you say?"

"He was further along than me. He was already on the other side. He was already living and dead. I wanted to see him on a large stage, recognize myself in him through the television. Like an enemy brother, a traitor who might finally extend his hand to me."

"But you were also afraid. I remember it well. You drew nearer to me. You warmed yourself up with me. You put a blanket over our legs, for a moment glued together, over our knees."

"I wasn't afraid. You're wrong. I was learning death from him . . . And I remembered, as I watched him, my years as a French soldier in Indochina."

"Indochina? You were in Indochina?"

"I fought for France during the war in Indochina."

"When?"

"A long time ago."

"With François Mitterrand?"

"No . . . It was atrocious. Atrocious. Atrocious. I killed so many people I didn't know, Asians who had done nothing to me . . . In Indochina, too, I wanted to leave the world for good. For someone to kill me. I wanted to disappear like my sister Zineb. Never come back. Vanish. Suddenly no longer exist. Somewhere find Zineb again at last . . ."

"You never forgot her, Zineb . . ."

"Zineb . . . Zineb . . ."

"And afterwards? Did you stay in Indochina for a long time?"

"The war ended . . . France tossed me aside, too . . . They sent me back to Morocco and forgot about me."

"You never received any retirement pay?"

"No."

"Was it François Mitterrand's fault?"

"Perhaps."

I would never understand that. But I tried.

Can death be learned?

To kill oneself, yes, I can conceive of that, see it in my

eyes: the steps to follow. The irrevocable decision. A small stool. A rope. The darkness. The end of the night, just before the voice of the muezzin who, alone, calls for the first prayer.

I see it all. What you did, Papa. I'm not angry at you. Don't worry.

The stool fell. I still hear the sound of that little fall. A dry sound, rapid, distinct, no echo.

THUD.

Life slips away. You rise up. You're no longer breathing. You learned how to do it. To do without. It doesn't take that much time.

I heard it, that THUD. I opened my eyes. I thought: It's just a cat passing by. I closed my eyes again. I fell back to sleep without even thinking of you.

You were just above. You were leaving the world.

The cat had passed.

I went back to sleep.

It was Friday. Holy day. White day.

They all cried.

Not me.

We hid the essential. The shame. We said: "A heart attack." I said it, too.

That night, on the terrace, where we were preparing the food for the funeral, Sawssane the Irish girl taught me something new.

She spoke differently. With a new voice.

"You will be alone from here on out, Zahira. It's true. It's true. I won't lie to you. But not forever. Through your mystic willpower, you will be able to maintain the connection with your father. Not by going to see sorcerers. No. By eating, simply by eating. In the sky, he will receive everything, he will eat with you what you've cooked while thinking of him. Your father gave you life. He did, not the heavens, not the gods, not the stars. You came from him. Now he is far, bring him back to you, to your body, to your breath. Eat him! Prepare very sweet mint tea. Make crêpes. Five. Drink all the tea. Eat all the crêpes. Each sip will be for him. Each bite, too. You will be two. You will live for him and for yourself. To achieve this miracle, it all comes down to that simple, trivial thing: food. Cooking, invested with a bit of yourself, your skin, your scent, your taste. You will be your father. He will be within you forever."

Yes, I am you, my father.

You died young. I died with you.

2. Before

TOMORROW, I'M CUTTING IT OFF. Do you hear me, Zahira? I'm going to do it. It's happening. God commands it. Not me. Do you still support me? Do you think I'm right? Tomorrow, I'm cutting it off completely. It will be erased. Disintegrated. I will not suffer. I will be asleep. In its place, I'll have something else.

An opening.

Dr. Johansson will do the operation. I trust him. He's not French. He's Swedish, from Stockholm. He told me himself. He's blond, of course. And handsome, very handsome, of course. Since starting the three-year-long procedure, I've fantasized about him, about what's under there when he lifts his little bright white doctor's smock. I don't know his first name. His last name is enough for me. Since the beginning of this week, every night I've repeated his name to fall asleep: Dr. Johansson. Dr. Johansson. Dr. Johansson. Dr. Johansson. Dr. Johansson. Come. Come. Come and cut it off of me. Oh, yes! Please! Please, Doctor!

I'm cutting it off. Do you hear me, Zahira? I don't want

it anymore. What a relief! What joy! To finally leave this cursed realm of men! Exit. Leave. Change. Finally reveal myself. Whether they like it or not. I will be other. Myself.

I'M CUTTING IT OFF.

No cock. No penis. No dick. No tumescence. No sperm. No balls. No useless thing between my legs that's ruined my life ever since I was born.

Do you understand? Do you find it funny? Laugh, then! Go on and laugh, Zahira! Forget your sadness! Forget your poor broke Parisian clients and laugh! What's wrong? Did you lower your prices yet again? Yes? Is that it? Poor thing! Poor thing! You're making me lose hope, truly . . . Pay attention, please! Don't distract me. In any event, your own problems will always be there. Let's stay focused on my big day.

Tomorrow, I'll be like you. Tomorrow, I'll have my revenge. Tomorrow, I'll screw them all. I won't abandon my hatred for them. Absolutely not. I will hold on to it. That's what allows me to survive still and always in this world of enraged dogs, assholes who are always thirsty. I will pamper it, my hatred. I will make a small mausoleum for it in my apartment. Just for my hatred. Are you still with me, Zahira? I'm right, aren't I? Hatred isn't a driving force for you, I know. It is for me. It has been forever and ever. If I could, I would kill them all. One after another. I would line them up against the wall. I would look them straight in the eyes. I would withdraw a bit, just a bit. And then I would give the signal to my army. My enemies would be shot in two, three seconds. I would witness their deaths, slow or rapid. Satisfied. True bliss, at last.

Ah, what a life, what sweet vengeance!

I've really earned it, my revenge. I paid for it. I gave everything. My skin. My cock. My ass. All the fantasies those clients had in their poor repressed heads, I made them come true. You know it, Zahira. You saw it firsthand. I broke my back from leaning over every night, hunched for hours, in the glacial cold of Porte Dauphine. Subjected to their mockery, their stupidity. Their cowardice.

My apartment, behind the Blanche metro stop, is mine. I worked like a tigress, a real she-devil, to have it. I slogged nonstop. I'm not like you. When the Yemeni sorcerer from Porte Saint-Denis offered me stronger, diabolical spells to attract more clients, I didn't hesitate. I said yes. I jumped at the chance. I didn't act pure, like you. Hesitant. Like someone who still has a heart, values. No. It would have been useless. They have to pay, all those men, those frustrated men, those men starving for dick, those assholes. I want all their money. All of it. The maximum amount of dough. I don't like them, in any event. Not in Algiers, where I was raped free of charge for years, and not here in this shithole that people still dare to call the most beautiful city in the world.

My ass! My shithole, too, sure, but not the most beautiful city in the world!

My apartment is magnificent. Jean-Jacques and Pierre decorated it well, and for free. I won't forget. But on the other hand, I did countless favors for those two Parisians over the years. I cooked them heaps of couscous and tagines. I brought them to the Barbès hammam numerous times and took perfect care of their bodies. Exfoliation.

Massage. Regularly, at least twice a week, I satisfied their overflowing libidos. A quickie with one. A blow job for the other. Two fingers in Jean-Jacques's ass. Just one, the thumb, in Pierre's. That was the only way they could come. And they say they're not passive . . . Yeah right! And I'm masculinity incarnate! You know them, too, Zahira. You know what I'm talking about. They call you up from time to time, for other services. I found out. There's no point in denying it. It doesn't bother me. That's between you and them. You know, that oh-so-Parisian French couple, who have completely forgotten the backcountry of the Vosges where they came from, are only still together because of me. I told you they're opposed to my operation. They've tried everything to dissuade me. They say that I'll regret it. That it's irreversible. That I'm not considering all the terrible consequences I'll have to deal with afterwards.

But what business is it of theirs?!

They act like intellectuals, those two queers. It's time for them to come back down to earth. Mr. Jean-Paul Sartre and la señora Simone de Beauvoir, it's over. It has been for a long time. Since even before the end of the last century. Do they realize it, you think? Do you speak with your clients about such things?

Sorry. I wasn't trying to make fun of you . . . All of France knows you specialize in humanitarian rescue. You only offer yourself to dirty, broke immigrants. Don't be so shocked, then, that you're still living in a 195-square-foot cage in Barbès. When I knew you, you were living in 97 square feet. Seventeen years later, you've doubled it! Bravo, Zahira! Bravo, Moroccan girl! Your compatriots must be ashamed of you. You're forty-five years old now, is that right?

Okay, okay, I'll stop acting like an idiot. But even so, I would like to know why you go to your Berber sorcerer from Gadir? And the Jew in Les Halles, do you still see him? Does he cast the spells that you really need? Don't you find that you're stagnating, that you're out of the loop and never stop to question yourself?

Answer me! Answer me!

Come on, come on, don't get angry. You know how much I love you. I just want what's best for you . . . All right . . . All right . . . Back to me. I'll talk about myself. It's better. It's more fun. Lighter. More festive. No? I'm the one who puts on a ton of makeup every night. Not you. I'm the one who wears miniskirts. Not you. I'm the one who wears wigs. Not you. And I'm the one who has more clients. Not you.

You're not saying anything. I've hurt you. You came to have tea with me and I turned our reunion into a trial. I'm sorry! It's just that I'm afraid for you, for your future. Everything passes, dies, so quickly. Money is the only thing that's real and eternal . . .

You're still not saying anything. I'm annoying you, is that it? Have some pastries. They're really good, don't you think? I bought them at La Bague de Kenza, as always. Take some home with you when you go . . .

Do you still see Hamdi the Egyptian? He's the one who gave me your news when you disappeared. He comes to see me regularly. Are you listening to me? Regularly. Another gay Arab man incapable of accepting himself. Honestly, what are they so afraid of? Do you know? It's just some ass. Two cocks meet, touch, come together, return to childhood together. It's easy to admit, to understand, no? We all want to fuck. Well, not everyone. I aspire to something else. But they, the others, the ones who take the metro, slave away the whole year for next to nothing, pay their taxes and the VAT, who believe they're freer than you and me, really, what are they so afraid of? That people call them fags because they come to see me? And? That people call them cocksuckers? Pedophiles? So what?

They disgust me. All of them. No. Not all of them. I have to be honest. Not all of them. Some of them are romantics, they just want to talk a little, laugh a little, share a tender kiss.

Others have pockets filled with money. We are here to take it from them. That's how it works. Some of them have houses in the countryside or near the sea. Where they send madame and the children. And they rush over to see me. I am ready. *Prêt. Prête.* Always. And nice and clean. Always. Even when I end up working the streets deep in Clichy, I never go out without my baby wipes. After each session, I clean myself properly, as one should, of their filth, of their perpetually denied frustrations. During the day, they revel in overblown language to describe the freedom they enjoy. And at night they come and hide with me and my Brazilian girlfriends. Do you understand it? You don't have anything to say about it? This market isn't your specialty. I know. What good does it do them, having all these laws, if it doesn't stop them from reproducing the same world, beautiful on the outside, and in reality so repressed. I would like to believe that their Joan of Arc really fought for freedom, and that their ancestors invented the rights of man. In 1789. But at the end of the day, what do we find here, in Paris, at the heart of the heart of France? The extremely inhibited bourgeoisie, too proud of their culture and always quite satisfied with themselves. Little tribes here, there, everywhere, that remind me of some of the people I knew in Algeria. The two sides, same difference. They think they're living in real freedom when they're only submitting to stronger forces, smarter minds.

Do you want the names of those French tribes? Louis Vuitton. Hermès. Dior. Chanel. The Louvre. The École normale supérieure, where those idiots Jean-Jacques and Pierre teach. The Panthéon, where they love to go bow down before their Greats. And then they dare to tell us that they're against slavery, that God doesn't exist, or whatever other bullshit.

Fine. I'll stop there. I'm acting like them. I'm overanalyzing. I'm citing names. References. I'm starting to get theoretical. That's not me, all of that. Let's get back to my cock. That's better.

Zahira. Zahira. I want a first name like yours. It sounds so good, Zahira. You are a *zahra*, my dear. A little flower. You are a *zhira*. A little breeze that smells like *zhar*. The orange blossom. You are the heart. Madness. Blood. That which brings happiness. And I know what I'm talking about. I know them all, here, your colleagues. Your sisters, as you call them sometimes. But only sometimes. You're not like them. The other girls gave up. You, in the end, didn't. You still believe that something will happen soon.

Your eyes have turned sad. But your soul still awaits a miracle.

You will be saved, Zahira. I always tell you that. I know you only half believe me. You're wrong.

The three-year procedure is over. I followed all of Dr. Johansson's instructions. I answered all the questions from the psychologists, psychiatrists, and gynecologists. I followed all their instructions to the letter.

Tomorrow, I'm cutting off my cock. And in the operating room, right before I surrender to the hands of the anesthetist, I will think only of you. I will not think of my mother. Nor of my father. Nor of those three men whom I loved purely. I will conjure you up before my eyes. I will renounce my manhood, my masculinity, using you as inspiration. Your body and its curves. Your scent that sets senses on fire. Your way of walking as if you were very slowly climbing a staircase. Your eyes that you never lower. Ever. You are not afraid. You fight. But you are always polite. Classy. I want to wake up as a woman with the same look I see in your eyes. Fixed. Sometimes hard, sometimes insolent. Always elegant. Where did you learn to use your eyes like that? Was it passed down to you by your father? By your big brother?

No, it's just you, that sad look, which somehow doesn't bring others down.

I want the same. The same. Is that okay with you? I know it's okay, my friend. My sister, possessed like me.

You have to pick me out a first name like yours. With a Z. And an *h*. And an *a*. The music that I hear in "Zahira," I want something like that.

What do you think? ZouZou, like the actress Soad Hosny in the Egyptian film *Watch Out for ZouZou*? Zineb, like your father's sister who disappeared somewhere a long time ago and who so fascinates me? Zahia, like your aunt who is alive and well? Zohra? Zhira? Zahra? Zannouba? You have seven names to choose from. Which one suits me best? Which one will help me be more like you? Tell me. Tell me. The last one? Tell me . . ."

"Zannouba. I like that name for you. Zannouba. Zannouba . . ."

"Why that one? It's missing an *h*. Answer me!"

"By becoming a woman tomorrow, you will be a bit more like me. But you will not be me. It's pointless to delude yourself. I don't want for you to catch even a little bit of my curse."

"You, Zahira, cursed?"

"Yes, that's what I am. That's what I see."

"You're wrong. A thousand times wrong. And you should change your mind-set. Maybe the others, the blind and unjust world, fling their insipid, nasty curses at you. Maybe. Trust me, none of it reaches you. You are far above them. Above everything."

"You see me with too much love, Zannouba."

"Zannouba! Thank you. Thank you. Thank you for already calling me by this new name. Real at last. Real through you, thanks to you. That's how I see it: a miracle and a curse at the same time. Okay, okay. In any event, I don't care. I want to be you, Zahira. I will be Zannouba through you. I already am. You have just confirmed it for me. You have baptized me. Thank you. From the bottom of my heart. Thank you for us all. Don't say anything. Don't answer anything. There is nothing more to say. Let me touch you. Take my head. Blow on my head. Shall we close our eyes? Go on! Go on! Did you do it? I did. I see nothing. I'll take some of your *baraka* . . . Open your eyes now, Zahira. Have some more tea and a small cake . . . Listen, Zahira, listen to me talk. I am Zannouba. This is the beginning of it all. Of all the stories of my life. The night that can never end. Words to invent. Identities to unveil . . . Are you still with me? Listen . . . Listen to me speak like Scheherazade. I'm turning back time. I'm going back to the beginning. Listen . . . Listen closely, Zahira . . ."

THE TEMPTATION OF THE LIPSTICK

They were all over me. A little eight-year-old boy. Happy. Seven sisters, all for me. They loved me. Took care of me. From head to toe. Several hands touched me. Cleaned me. Pampered me. Massaged me. Coated me with oils and cheap perfumes. I let them do as they pleased every time, without ever closing my eyes. Hands, overexcited and joyous, mixed, mingled, fought over my little body.

It happened quietly in the beginning. Nothing heavy. We were preparing the event. We were concentrating. We were on the green rug, in the guest room.

Winter or summer, it was always the same ritual. My sisters seemed to obey inaudible orders they alone could understand.

They had to sacrifice me. They knew what to do. How to transform me. All enter into me, become me, turn me into the link with the heavens.

We hid for the ceremony. We locked the front door to the house. We made sure our mother was off to the souk. There was no one. Only my sisters and me.

I was happy without shame: a dream. I am the only boy on earth. I am the only girl on earth.

That's what happened: the Event. Transform. Be reborn. Return to the source. I didn't question it.

7 girls + 1 boy = 8 girls.

1 brother + 7 sisters = 8 sisters.

The rule of numbers. It's logic.

I witnessed my own transformation. It wasn't magic. It was real.

My sisters supplied everything. Our mother's green caftan. Our aunt Batoule's yellow scarf. The blue babouches belonging to Saâdia, our eldest sister.

Three colors: green for the body, yellow around the head, and feet in blue.

Radiant, that little army prepared to carry out the large-scale operation.

The face. Very simple. Three hardly noticeable touches. Kohl on the eyes. Deep red lipstick on the lips. And a bit of powder on the cheeks.

The sisters stepped back. At a bit of a distance, seated, they formed a complete circle around the light.

They were waiting.

It was my turn.

I stood up.

I offered myself up to the gaze of one sister after another. I greeted them softly, lovingly. Recognizing myself in each of them.

7. Magic number. Odd. I am the 8 that completes it. And extends it towards the 9. I am at the same time the 8 and the 9.

Incubated by the free and benevolent gazes of my sisters, I fly, I surpass the limits of this world. And I extend my arm. One after another, they plant a kiss on my hand.

I was a little boy. Now I am a little girl. King and queen. I come back down to earth.

One of my sisters lets out a *youyou*. Then a second. And a third. It heightens our joy. Our shining eyes will shatter with happiness.

My transformation continues. I start to sing.

My sisters sing, too. Our voices mix together marvelously.

I dance. As a girl.

I dance. As a boy.

Our happiness is enormous. No one can take it from us. Our union is eternal. My sisters are mine, they will never marry. Laws aren't made for us. Unanimously, we stop recognizing them. President Boumediene is no longer our president. I am the Master. The Mistress. The little god. I am convinced of it.

When I was born they named me Aziz. "Dear one." I am. With them. With their blessing, I become Aziza.

Aziz. Aziza. I think both. As I continue to sing and dance, I mingle them.

And I fall. Without hurting myself. I am a body on earth, in ecstasy. My sisters approach me. They devour me with kisses.

I still hear them, those noisy kisses.

They stopped when I was about thirteen years old.

Suddenly I had to remain Aziz and only Aziz.

My unhappiness began in that moment, when they told me that childhood had finished and it was time to wear the mask of a man. It wasn't advice. It was an order repeated every day and every night.

Very soon after, the sisters left one after another. They were married off. They were given to strange men who lived elsewhere, far, very far away.

I didn't see them again, my sisters.

I didn't forget them. Every morning and every night, I said their names.

Saâdia. Hakima. Saïda. Fathia. Halima. Maryam. Nadia.

I remained alone.

I am alone. No joy. No magic. No innocence.

They had shown me the path. The world destroyed it all. Brutal men stole, kidnapped my sisters. They rape them, I know, over and over. My sisters can't say anything.

Now my sisters have children. But I don't want to know them. I don't want to know anything about them anymore, about their new lives.

The shock of our separation destroyed me. I could no longer speak, eat, relish life. Without the bodies of my sisters around me, meaning was lost, the light gone out forever.

One night, I made the decision: to no longer exist. I would no longer be an Algerian. Nor an Arab. Nor a Muslim. Nor an African. None of it.

I turned hard. A monster. A degenerate. No purpose, no battle to fight.

It was obvious that I was receding from the world, but no one extended their hand to me.

Later, many years later, I realized the true weight of my tragedy, understood what they had taken from me, into what cold hell they had forced me. I remember that day very clearly.

It was the day the temptation to wear red lipstick came back.

I was with a client, the last one, at the end of the night. Porte Dauphine. The routine. Beyond exhaustion. The man was doing his business in my behind. I felt nothing. I was trying to think of a song by Warda. "Khalik Hena." "Stay Here."

The client's pelvic thrusts sped up. I was losing hope. I couldn't recall that song. But I continued to search in that bygone time, back in Algeria.

And it came. Came back. Just a small part:

> Stay here, stay.
> What's the point of leaving on a trip.
> You say: Only two days!
> And you leave for a year.
> What's the point of leaving on a trip.
> I'm afraid of tomorrow
> And of what will happen
> As soon as you leave.
> You will leave us for an entire year.
> And you will leave behind a wounded love.

As I'm very softly humming those two last words, "wounded love," *habib mjrouh,* suddenly the buried past came back to the surface. It spurted up through a specific desire: the temptation to wear red on my lips. A fake Chanel lipstick, probably made in China. I needed that one and no other. I had to find it quickly, it was like a life-threatening emergency, my childhood, the joy among my sisters, me as a glorious child, through the magic of the cheap lipstick my sisters had used.

I had just arrived in Paris. I prostituted myself dressed as a moderately savage Arab boy from over there, Algeria. The clients liked that, liked for me to smell like my home country, the savagery of the village, as they liked to say.

The client was going to come in my ass soon. I arched my back slightly. That excited him even more. I looked at the sky searching for the sign that would appear, I was sure of it.

The client ejaculated noisily in me. My favorite moment, one of the reasons I was in the profession. It was hot, sweet, nourishing. I felt this regular client's sperm burrow through me, wind its way in, leave its mark everywhere.

Thus sustained and rekindled, I had the strength, the power, to read the sign showing me where to go to buy my sisters' lipstick, Chanel, fake and cheap.

Tati.

That's where I went the very next day, Tati in Barbès. Our version of Printemps, our Galeries Lafayette, isn't that right, Zahira?

Isn't that right?

Zahira! Zahira! Zahira! Did you fall asleep? Are you really sleeping?

Why should I continue with my story, then?

Sleep. You're missing the most important part: that moment when, after I had found the lipstick, I understood that I had to return to the past, pick up where the story had left off, in Algeria, when I was thirteen.

Leave behind my cock, my gender, men, be a woman. Be one of my sisters. With them. Far from them. Cut off all that is masculine in me to become them. Reconcile myself with the glorious little child I had once been. Listen to him. Realize his dream. His true nature. Love him again, at last.

Tomorrow, at the end of the day, I will go to the Hôpital Saint-Louis. They will take me into the operating room at 7:30 p.m. At nine o'clock Dr. Johansson will begin the operation.

They will cut it off of me.

You will be with your nightly clients, Zahira.

You will think of me. Right? You will think of me. You have to. Because I will no longer have access to anything, neither to myself nor to my body. Nor my hopes.

Think of me. Pray for me, in your own way.

You're all I have left, Zahira.

3. In the Center

I LOVE PARIS. It's my city. I don't have a French passport but no one can contest this right. This belonging. Paris is my city, my kingdom, my path. This is where I always wanted to come. To flee. To grow up. To learn about the world freely. Walk without fear, anywhere. Walk. Keep walking. Become a whore. Officially. Embrace it.

This is where I want to die. This is where I want to write my testament. I will bequeath all that I have to the caretaker's son. They're from a suburb of Lille. They are so poor. She has only him. He has only her.

He's barely nine years old. He's named Antoine. I am in love with him.

Antoine: little charming French bird.

Antoine: little cherub with his little wings showing.

Antoine: genius and magician.

He understands everything, Antoine, he guessed my profession on his own. When his mother sends him to give me the mail, he looks at me, kindly. He doesn't say a word. I crouch down. He kisses me on both cheeks, very slowly.

His skin is like milk. I don't need to lick it to know what it tastes like, its sweetness and its saltiness. I look at Antoine. Antoine looks at me.

He, too, will ask me for something, later on, when he's a bit older. I won't refuse him anything. I will open my tender arms.

I like his name. I like his way of setting down one foot after another. I like when I happen upon him, sometimes, sitting on the steps in the stairwell, crying. I don't interrupt him. I let his tears stream out until there are no more. Once, only once, he told me why he was crying.

"Rex is dead, Zahira! He's dead!"

"Who's Rex, Antoine?"

"The dog . . . my aunt's . . . in Lille . . . He's dead."

"When did he die?"

"A month ago."

"And you just found out?"

"No . . . I've known for a month . . ."

I sat down next to him. He continued to cry. Then he placed his head on my leg.

"Rex is dead."

I would remember that short sentence all my life.

Antoine gave me the most beautiful thing, the rarest thing. A precious and pure memory.

That dog Rex had been dead for several weeks already. Antoine, a little being, six years old at the time, had just understood, had just realized something. The feeling of loss. The need for a solitary corner in which to take refuge. The hope of being unburdened, consoled, loved, by someone.

In my will, there is only him.

There will only be him. Antoine, it's Paris from here on out for me. Paris and life.

I've lived in this city for seventeen years. I should hate it, curse it, abandon it. Go elsewhere: join my girlfriends who make a fortune in Switzerland, in Geneva and Zurich especially. They're constantly calling me up. Apparently there aren't enough girls over there. Moroccan women have a lot of success with Swiss men, who are always so generous with them. But money doesn't interest me. That's not my driving force, what compels me to spread my legs for clients. And I don't have many of them, I'll admit it. What does it matter. In my building there is Antoine: that's what's important. And two metro stops away there's Iqbal: my Sri Lankan.

My love.

I committed a grave error with him. After meeting him and declaring my love to him, I continued to practice my profession. One day, I slept with two of his friends, without realizing they knew each other. A week later, they saw me with him in his wash-and-fold on the Rue des Martyrs.

Of course, they told him everything.

Iqbal immediately cut off all contact with me. He even changed his cell phone number.

The situation was critical. I had to swallow my pride and go on the counterattack.

But I let a week go by before showing up one night at his wash-and-fold.

Iqbal was doing the books. He loves it, money, moolah. And, bizarrely, that's what I love about him. His organized and always forward-thinking side.

I know that he would absolutely make a very good father.

I fell in love with him. I want to force him to marry me and for us to quickly have children together. I still have about two years ahead of me to accomplish these two miracles. I'm forty years old. Apparently we can still have kids even at forty-five. If we've had children in the past. Which is not the case for me. But anyway, Iqbal will open everything for and in me. With him, I'll become a mother. I'm sure of it. Period, the end.

Of course, as soon as he saw me cross the threshold, he was very nice, very courteous. As usual, he drew the blinds. And we made love on the floor, madly: an endless explosion.

That's the other source of my passion for that handsome Sri Lankan. When it comes to sex, we were put on this earth to be together. One in the other.

He willingly lets me dominate him, play with him, use him, lick him, bite him, twist him every which way. And for him to come, he always wants me to penetrate him. A finger. Sometimes two. Thanks to the tips from my Algerian friend Aziz, I've learned how to do it perfectly, slowly, gently.

I know all about how my Iqbal functions sexually. All his secrets, his shames.

I rarely come with him. But that's not at all important. I can manage it on my own when I want, where I want.

Iqbal needs me. I'm the only one who understands him. And on top of it, I'm Muslim and Arab. Which is to say: the ultimate fantasy for Sri Lankans, Pakistanis, Indians, and their cousins. A Muslim with whom Iqbal is not afraid to let go, to open himself up completely.

And I like that. When Iqbal becomes my little woman. And after, once we've finished, he becomes a man again. The man.

Iqbal is a man in any event, no doubt about it. It's enough to see him walk in the street, look down on people, speak to them with a natural authority, snub them sometimes, give them only what he wants to give them. In the ranking of immigrants in France, he is all the way at the bottom. But he doesn't care. The white French people are too arrogant, they don't intimidate him at all.

He is never afraid.

He always carries himself like a king. The king of Paris. Perhaps I'm exaggerating a bit about that. Let's say: the king of the Sri Lankans of Paris. Besides, after not even ten years here, he already owns five wash-and-folds and five laundromats.

Iqbal is rich. And that's the third reason pushing me to accept everything. With him, I wouldn't have to prostitute myself anymore. I would be the wife of the king. That said, I still have a long way to go.

After we made love on the cold floor, Iqbal gave me his verdict, in four sentences:

"I knew that all Moroccan girls were whores. But I didn't know that you were one of them. My friends Ramzee and Salman told me that they slept with you. And that they definitely paid you."

That's all. Not a word more.

I denied everything, of course. Absolutely everything.

"A whore! Are you insane, Iqbal?"

He stared at me. I didn't lower my gaze, obviously. The

stare-down lasted nearly a minute. I needed some doubt to insinuate itself into his mind.

I thought I had succeeded in my mission. I was wrong.

That night Iqbal brought me to a Turkish restaurant, his favorite, on Rue du Faubourg-Saint-Denis. We didn't speak another word about our argument. Instead we laughed, a lot, and ate, abundantly. We separated late in the night without making any promises.

I watched Iqbal turn around and walk down the street. Terrified, I watched him grow distant, disappear.

I didn't sleep that night, of course. In my head I went over all the options still at my disposal to keep Iqbal in my life.

Since then, it's been a total impasse.

He still needs me sexually. He comes to see me once every two weeks. We do the deed. He takes off again. Without a word.

Sometimes, when he hasn't visited in a month, I go to the wash-and-fold. He never says anything. He pulls down his pants. We do what we have to do. And I leave.

I'm sure he's in love with me. How could he not be?

Over time, I have become an expert at satisfying his every desire, including those even he isn't fully aware of.

Now I have a plan that I'm refining very patiently. I will not give up Iqbal. Never. I'm not Moroccan for nothing.

I've always been told, ever since I was little, that men never marry their sexual fantasy. It's not worth trying. That's the reality the world over, by all accounts. Men marry women who remind them of their mothers, not women who make them get hard, orgasm.

All right then. We'll just see about that!

Iqbal is already mine. He just doesn't know it yet. He belongs to me in heart, body, soul, and cock. He was created for me. Only for me.

I will have him, no matter what. One day he will put a very expensive ring on my finger, one day very soon. I'm working on it. Very seriously.

I have three sorcerers. One, Jewish, in Paris for emergencies. A second, a Berber, in Gennevilliers. A third, Moroccan, in Azilal, in the Atlas Mountains: he's my favorite, the one who understands me the best, who lets me tell him everything, even the crudest, most sordid details. The only problem with him is that he lives far from Paris, in the heart of Morocco. I can't see him very often. I'm going to bring him over here very soon, on a tourist visa. One month in my building. There's a furnished studio on the second floor that I'll rent for him, so that he can perform the necessary sorcery. One month devoted exclusively to breaking Iqbal, finally making him do what I want.

My sorcerer in Azilal is tired of working on Iqbal from a distance, and I am, too. But I call him often to keep him apprised of the situation and get his thoughts.

Iqbal is still attached to me, I see it clearly, through his cock and through something else: love, I'm sure of it. But I want more, I need more: to become his wife. If not, what good is it to slave away from morning to night, welcome all the third-class immigrants of Paris between my legs? As if by magic, they all find me, knock at my door. And often, they don't have a lot of money, not the amount I ask them for in any case. I never dare to send them back home frustrated. So I sacrifice myself, in a sense. I put on an Oum Kalthoum song and lie down. Without getting fully undressed, they jump on top of me, plunge into me, forget themselves in me, in the heat of my sex.

As strange as it must seem, I always feel a certain pleasure with them. Not quite sexual. More a pleasure of tenderness, of slightly assuaged distress and hunger. I feel like a sister to these Arab and Muslim men.

It's become my specialty. The Arab or Muslim men of Paris. Most of them undocumented. Most of them used by this city that mistreats them with no remorse, and by their white French bosses who exploit them under the table without a hint of guilt.

Turks. Egyptians. Tunisians. Algerians. Indians. Moroccans, too, but rarely. Some washed-up men from the Gulf countries.

My preference, by far, is for Pakistanis. Iqbal doesn't look like Sri Lankan men. He's more like a Pakistani. A little harsher than them, though.

The Pakistani men of Paris are the sweetest men on earth. Well raised. Polite. I never ask them to wash themselves. I like their scent, their smooth mannerisms, their timidity, their murmurs.

I don't understand their language. They don't understand Arabic and speak very poor French. They are different from my Arab clients even though they're also Muslim. But the Muslim faith is far more inspiring on them. So beautiful, rare. The Pakistanis, in my eyes, have best preserved that Muslim quality. What makes Islam Islam.

Sometimes, I don't even ask them to pay. Watching them

do with me as they please is more than enough for me. It's like going to the theater, to the cinema, to see a show with your favorite actor, not the one who excites you sexually, no, the one who inspires you, who lifts you up. That's what I find with the Pakistanis. Peace. Paradise. Love that needs no words.

If only Iqbal could be like them. A pure angel.

My young Jewish sorcerer in Les Halles has told me many times that such a transformation is possible. I like him a lot. He's named Samuel, a very pretty name. He's funny. I think he's a little bit gay. Maybe even very gay. But, unfortunately, he's not a great sorcerer. Which is a huge shock for me. In Morocco, the Jewish sorcerers are the most powerful beings in the world.

My sorcerer in Gennevilliers isn't very professional. As soon as he sees me, he gets hard. And as a result, he can't concentrate on his work: to communicate with jinns. Not that one necessarily has to be pure to call on them, to wake them, but all the same it's recommended not to have an erection when you do so. Otherwise, everything gets scrambled. And that's what's happened each of the last few times.

So?

So the only one I have left is my sorcerer from the village, from Azilal. He will arrive in two weeks.

I've worked very hard recently. I've even taken on whites, old Arabs from Belleville who no longer know what to do with their lives, and young Moroccan students, sometimes rich, who prowl around the Montparnasse train station without knowing how to approach those horrible little French minxes, who are in reality quite dull. I've expanded my hunting territory all the way to Rue du Faubourg-Saint-Denis, where there are also Kurds, Afghans, and even some Shiite Iraqis.

I've earned a decent amount of money.

And before the *haj* from Azilal arrives, I can still work a few areas near the Champs-Élysées, in the oriental cabarets invaded by the new generation of Moroccan prostitutes, those who have just arrived in France and who still dream big. All the way to the sky. Meaning, a loaded man from the Gulf. Or even a prince. They know, as I know, that there are a decent number of members of the royal family from those countries who come to have fun and chase easy Moroccan girls in Paris.

I'm beyond old, compared to them. I don't care. I have to accumulate the maximum amount of cash. The *haj* from Azilal will stay here for one month. It'll cost me a lot of money. Who knows, I could finally hit the jackpot . . .

All this for Iqbal. All this for love and its madness. All this to no longer be alone.

I'm tired of telling myself the same fantasies every night. I'm tired of feeling numb between my legs at the end of the day. Because I have to take them, all those super-hard cocks, so forceful and so impatient.

I'm tired of not achieving anything concrete. I give. I give. Nothing real. Nothing for later. A husband. A marriage. A house. Peace. Staying at home. Pretending to be submissive. Hiring a maid or two. Giving them orders. Directing my world without budging from my couch. And, most importantly, getting fat. Eating enough to develop generous, overflowing curves.

I know that Iqbal will adore me like that, as a woman who's fully embraced domestic life, fleshy and delicious.

He can pay for me to have that life. He has more than enough to make my happiness, my dreams, a reality. He is the only one who can heal my profound discontentment with life, rid me of the bitterness and sourness that are gradually settling into me. I am ready to give him everything. He can make me into a slave if he wants. Mistreat me if he wants. I'll take everything. Everything. As long as he comes. Gives in. And he'll see what will happen.

I will make him change worlds. God. Family. He will be my thing, my hit, my *kif.* My legal man. My *hallal* man.

I know that I don't ask for much from life, from God. I know it. I want only Iqbal, so that I can start the final chapter of my existence with him. Nothing more.

A few weeks ago, I went to see my friend Aziz. It was the night before he was going to have an important operation. He's changing sex. As usual, once again he wanted me to tell him the story of the disappearance of Zineb, my father's sister. The mystery surrounding that woman obsesses him much more than it does me. He recognizes himself in her act. She was here. She is no longer here. And as usual, we watched an entertaining Bollywood movie. We love everything that comes from India. Then we spoke about our plans and our unhappiness. He told me of his sad past and the origin of his desire to become a woman. And to distract him, I told the story of Naïma, my former best friend in Paris. Her life was very similar to mine. Like her, I wait, hopeful. I know that miracles happen. They exist. They exist. I see them. Iqbal cannot let me down.

Just at the moment when everything was drawing to a close for Naïma, the doors suddenly opened. Wide. Very wide.

I told that story as if it were a legend. Fascinated, excited, Aziz listened to me with eyes full of recognition.

THE HAPPY TALE OF NAÏMA

"I was right not to give up. My destiny was finally fulfilled, it found a new path, its own path, true from the beginning. There was a meaning to that tortured, dull life, wrecked long ago. I had to pass through the immense desert to find my oasis at last. Don't ever turn your back on your goal, Zahira. You will attain your salvation. The wish of a sincere heart will always be granted."

Naïma has good reason to talk like that.

She ended up finding a place to rest, to abandon herself, to no longer be dry and sour.

Her words are permeated with a somewhat naïve philosophy, but they are so sincere. She is finally speaking her own language, the one deep within her that no one saw before.

Naïma comes from far away. Very far away. She's fifty years old today. And, thank God, she did not become a good Muslim woman, like so many others at the end of their career. She doesn't want to go to Mecca to wash away her sins. No. No. She considers having been a prostitute for all those long years as being more than enough for her to enter paradise upon her death. She was a better Muslim than so many others who talk your ear off with their fake piety.

Naïma laughs today. She eats. She sends money to her brothers in Casablanca. From afar she watches over the grave of her mother, buried in their home village, near El Jadida.

She forgave me. Years ago, when I had just arrived in Paris, I stole her clients all the time. I didn't know how to get my own yet.

Naïma told me, last week:

"I saw everything, Zahira, and I let you do it. One day you would understand on your own and repent. There is nothing to forgive, little sister. You did what you had to do. And hey, stealing is an art, too."

Tears began to stream from my eyes. She was no longer Naïma. She had become a saint. A true saint. I got down on my knees and kissed her feet. She put two hands on my head. She raised me up. She brought her face close to mine and placed a tender kiss on my grateful lips.

She gave me her *baraka*.

"The dark path can lead somewhere. Hell might be eternal, yes, but at a certain point it stops being only hell. It transforms. We adapt. Something in us opens. The miracle happens. It has to happen."

Naïma spoke like a prophet. I told her that. She laughed in my face.

"I am neither prophetess nor poetess, and even less a pure soul. Don't change how you think of me. I am a whore like you. Well, I'm not anymore. But I don't renounce any part of my past. Don't change, Zahira. We don't change. We move forward. We go and, one day, things come together, align. Make sense. Or not. So, please, don't treat me like the woman I have not become . . . You know what happened to me, don't you?"

Of course I knew.

At the end of her career as a prostitute, no one wanted to lend Naïma a hand, save her from decline. She went to ruin, alone, in Paris, a city that she too adores.

After babysitting, a profession that doesn't pay much, for the horrendous bourgeois of the sixteenth arrondissement, she became a barmaid at a place for old Arabs who still hadn't gotten over the shock of having given away their youth, their strength, their soul, for France, a country more than unappreciative of them, and yet a country they couldn't seem to leave.

Naïma's decline went on for two years in that seedy bar near the Goncourt metro stop, opposite the church . . . She let herself go. At night, after closing, she would offer herself to nearly anyone who still wanted her. For nothing.

Impossible to believe that this destroyed woman was the same one who had begun her career in the luxury hotels of Casablanca, Beirut, Cairo, and London. She who had turned heads, chosen whom she wanted, set her own prices higher than the going rate, was now a rag that was too yellow, too wrung out, too frayed, ready for the trash.

Her story gives me hope. Somewhere, in this winter, on this always-cold earth, beyond the earth, there is a great heart for every man, every woman, for all of us.

Being a barmaid didn't pay Naïma enough to cover everything: rent, phone, bills, taxes, school tuition for her nieces and nephews in Morocco, her African sorcerer who regularly organized séances to gently appease the jinns that inhabited her. She needed more money to satisfy everyone who depended on her, who couldn't continue to survive without her help.

Naïma has a lot of brothers and sisters who found themselves in the same situation. It's their destiny, our destiny: to pay with our bodies for the futures of others.

Barmaid in the evening and into the night. Maid at a hotel in the fifteenth arrondissement, near the Convention metro stop. That's how she got by, more or less.

The owner of the hotel was Algerian.

Later, once they were married, he told her that he had fallen in love with her when they first met. At first sight.

She didn't believe him. He never stopped swearing it to her. Love, immediately.

In reality, Naïma spent only two months at that hotel. It was too tiring. Backbreaking. She preferred to go back to babysitting while continuing her work at the bar.

Two years later, the Algerian came to have a drink at the bar where she was still working at night.

"You don't remember me?"

"No."

"You're sure?"

"I'm sure."

"Look closely . . . Am I nice?"

"Yes, very nice."

"Are you mocking me?"

"Just a little bit."

"You don't remember nice men?"

"I haven't come across any for a long time. I think that's all over now."

"What's over?"

"Nice people."

"I'm a nice man."

"I believe you."

"You should believe me . . . Naïma . . ."

"You know me? You know my name?"

"I never forgot it."

"Stop pulling my leg."

"I'm serious, Naïma. I'm the Algerian who runs the Hôtel Astoria where you worked two years ago. Do you see now?"

"I see, yes . . . I see . . ."

"That makes me happy."

"Excuse me?"

"You're not going to ask my name?"

"What's your name?"

"My name is Jaâfar."

"Nice to meet you, Jaâfar. I'm Moroccan."

"I know, Naïma."

"You want a glass of wine? On me . . ."

"I didn't come here for that . . . I don't drink in any case."

"Why are you here, then?"

"To see you. To find you again. Ask you something."

"What?"

"Say my name . . . Please . . ."

"Jaâfar."

"One more time."

Jaâfar had truly fallen in love with Naïma from the first day they met. Madly in love. But he hadn't said anything to her at the time. He was married. His wife was dying in the hospital. He knew perfectly well what was happening to him, the love that was making its way into his heart with a loud bang.

He didn't hesitate to do what needed to be done. Accompany his wife to the end, to the door of the sky. Not disavow her while she was still alive.

So he revealed nothing to Naïma, didn't let her see a thing.

Two years later, after his wife died, he sold everything he owned in Paris: the hotel and three apartments. He wound up with a nice little fortune. He shared half of it between his two children, who each had their own families.

And he set out to find Naïma.

Jaâfar wasn't really an old man. He was only fifty-six.

Naïma considered herself finished, one of the living dead, when the Algerian found her again. What he told her, in the sordid bar where she was drowning in her misery, more than surprised her. She had a hard time believing him.

She told him so. Jaâfar's short response shook her and, at the same time, opened up something new in her.

Jaâfar said:

"I might be a liar, but here, before you, I am speaking the truth. For more than two years, I've dreamed about you day and night. You have to believe me."

He said it in Arabic, with an Algerian accent.

Naïma's heart suddenly softened without her permission.

Never before had anyone made a sincere declaration of love to this woman.

She was happy. Of course. She couldn't think of anything to say to Jaâfar. She simply lowered her eyes. And she let a tear run down her cheek. Jaâfar got up and, courageously, dared to dry that tear. The Arabs who were in the bar that night couldn't believe their eyes. One of them applauded. A second. The whole bar.

Naïma says that miracles happen. Now her family is proud of her.

Naïma brought Jaâfar to Casablanca. They had a big wedding. They bought a house in El Jadida, Naïma's birthplace. But both of them love Paris. That's where they dream of going to try their luck till the very end.

I don't know if I want to be like Naïma. I'll never have her luck. But I believe in her miracle.

And, like her, each morning I tell myself that no matter what happens, Paris is mine. Ours. Yours, too, Aziz.

Do you agree?

PART II
Paris, August 2010

1. In the Clouds

I AM A WOMAN. I became a woman. It's been two months now.
I'm talking to myself.

Without looking at myself in the mirror, I know, I am the changes that are taking place in me. And I am talking.

I see no one. I don't want to see the monster I have become reflected in the eyes of others. Their fake comprehension. Their pity. Their unease. Their forced kindness. So I distance myself from everyone. I stay alone in this overly large apartment, decorated in an overly French style by my friends Jean-Jacques and Pierre. Even Zahira, I don't want her to visit very often. Twice a week. No more. She buys groceries for me. Prepares my food for the next several days. Cleans what needs to be cleaned. Tidies what needs to be tidied. Gives me three kisses on each cheek before leaving. Calls me by my new name.

Zannouba.

"Zannouba" comes out of Zahira's mouth as though it were obvious. A smile that comes from far away. Me in a past life. Once more in the reality of the world.

Apart from Zahira, the others can go to hell. I don't need their solidarity, or their support. Let them keep their good wishes and their bullshit to themselves.

What I need is a gaze that is true, free, that doesn't judge me, that sees me and nothing more.

Zahira. Always and forever her. Zahira is the only one capable of that. A hand on my forehead. A kiss on my hand. A word that makes me come to life again. *Khti*. My sister.

I believe her.

I've always believed her. Even when she makes fun of me, I stick with her through her outbursts and her sadness.

Zahira understands that I don't want people to call me right now. There's nothing to say. The operation happened. They changed my sex.

I should feel like a woman. Be happy. Joyous. Throw a party. Be light, as before. As in my dreams from before.

The opposite is happening to me.

I cry day and night. Night and day.

Below, between my legs, what was heavy, cumbersome, is gone.

They cut it off. In me, in its place, there is an opening. But I feel nothing.

Nothing.

Air enters. Passes. I should shiver. Tremble. But no. Nothing.

I don't hear anything below.

Even when I piss, there aren't those little delicate noises I was expecting. In its place, a strong stream of water. It comes out, strong. As before, strong. It's not a woman pissing. No.

Great despair.

I go to the bathroom countless times per day. I try to solidify my idea of womanhood through that ordinary, repeated act. I try to summon up sonorous memories of my mother pissing freely, with no shame. Rediscover that particular sound.

TSSSSSTSSSSSTSSSSS.

Impossible! I never succeed.

The yellow water that flows from me is like a torrent. It's pushed out and surges with a powerful energy that I know too well and in which I never recognized myself. Like a waterfall in the middle of a river.

I'm ashamed.

I stop pissing. I hold my head in my hands.

I've become a woman. On the outside. The cock and balls are gone, I buried them myself. Deep down, all the way down, there is still, and there will no doubt remain, a current of masculinity that was always more than foreign to me.

For years, as soon as I made a bit of money in Paris, I did everything I could to mask that intruding manliness. Creams. Makeup. Clothes. Waxing. Wigs. Shoes with incredibly high stiletto heels. Hormones. Injections.

That hid things, somewhat. Never completely. I don't understand. I don't understand.

What happens inside me escapes me.

I obeyed my deep nature, what I always felt inside my secret heart: I am not a boy, I am a girl.

I had to have the operation. This change that wasn't one. Not to go from boy to girl. To become the girl I had always been, long before I came into the world.

Now that it's happened, the obvious transformation, the more-than-necessary repair, I find myself unsatisfied again. Completely overwhelmed by the manly side that still runs through me, in my veins, that dominates my genes.

What am I going to do now?

I can't go to the bathroom anymore. I don't want to anymore. And to avoid needing to piss, I've decided to stop drinking water.

Little by little, I wither. Body. Heart. Spirit. I no longer know what to do nor how to do it.

Am I a woman, completely a woman?

No.

Am I still a man?

No.

Who am I, then?

I don't regret anything that I've done. I wanted this operation. This disappearance, I'm the one who planned it, orchestrated it. Brought it to fruition. I thought of everything. But not of the essential: how to be a woman? I mean, beyond clothing and makeup, what is a woman?

Why, before the operation, did I know all the answers to these questions? And now: nothing?

Each day I lose the joy from before, this desire from before that gave me a reason for existing. Revealing my true identity. Making all the sacrifices for it to happen. Not a miracle but reality, just reality. The project of a life becoming concrete, true.

Was it a mistake?

In my huge bed, I no longer know how to calm myself

down, reassure myself with dependable, definitive answers that will never come.

I'm in the void. I can't manage to fill it.

Who to imitate? Who to model myself after? Where to find good advice, the word that makes things right, the gesture that reconciles, the look that loves without expecting anything in return? Where?

Who will guide me?

No one talks about what's happening to me in this moment. No one has dared to describe this territory where one is no longer at all defined. Where one is outside of every category, yesterday's and today's.

What to do with myself now? I can't stop turning the question over in my head, and now it has nothing to grab onto.

Why not go to a bookstore and look for a book that really addresses this subject, me in this moment, without a condescending voice, without too many empty theories?

That book doesn't exist.

And films? There has to be one that addresses situations like mine. I'm sure of it. But which one? I should call Dr. Johansson. He'll tell me. Except he must still be on vacation. What to do, then? Who to call for help? Zahira only knows and only likes Indian movies. She's basically a specialist in the genre, she can always find something that sweeps her off her feet, makes her believe that other lives are possible elsewhere.

I think of the little Algerian boy who didn't feel like a boy. Among girls, his sisters, he would open up, he would laugh, he would dance, he was in heaven.

I see now what he's become. He's in purgatory.

He. Her. Is it true?

"What if I called my sisters?"

"Yes, that's it . . . That's a good idea, Zannouba. Call them all, right away, tell them that you've become like them, exactly like them . . . Go on . . . Go on . . . Go ahead . . . Be brave! Embrace your new condition! Call them, they'll be able to comfort you . . . Go ahead . . . Go ahead, for goodness' sake!"

"You're wrong, Aziz. Your sisters can't do anything for you. You know what Algerian society has turned them into: veiled women, slaves to their cowardly husbands. The living dead."

"Are you listening to what you're saying, Zannouba? What do you know of their lives, of their day-to-day, of their problems? You really think that just because they're veiled, they've automatically lost their liberty!"

"Yes, I do."

"Don't make me laugh! You're talking like all those sanctimonious Westerners, now. To comfort themselves, prove to themselves that they're the ones in the right, they seek examples in other places of people who, according to them, lack freedom . . . Arab women, for example."

"But they're right. Arab women lack freedom. That's the reality."

"Are you listening to what you're saying? What's going on with you?"

"That's exactly the problem . . . I don't know what's going on with me."

"You wanted to become a woman?"

"Yes."

"You are one."

"You think?"

"You are one, I'm telling you. You are an Arab woman . . ."

"You're making fun of me!"

"Not at all. You're right to think of your sisters in Algeria. In your memories of them, you will find salvation. The example to follow."

"Veil myself like them?"

"Why not?"

"Are you serious?"

"*Sérieuse*, you mean. I'm you—have you forgotten? My wee-wee's gone, just like yours."

"You regret it, it seems."

"Yes, a bit. I'll admit it."

"I don't regret it at all. Not at all."

"You're lying. As usual, you're lying. The truth is right in front of you and you refuse to see it. That's so typical of you! Fleeing. Always fleeing. Now, you have to own it, poor thing. You wanted to become the woman you always believed you were deep down? Well, look at yourself in the mirror: you are, you've succeeded. You're beautiful. You're magnificent. Ravishing. The Parisians are going to adore you. Make you into an example of a liberated Arab, who's not ashamed. Not like the others, those from the village, who're still rotting in ignorance and submission. You've succeeded, my dear! Bravo! Bravo!"

"Enough! Enough!"

"I'm not afraid of you anymore."

"Enough, I said!"

"Are you threatening me? You can't do anything to me now . . . You're a wreck . . . A lowlife, the lowest . . ."

"Enough!"

"You're nothing . . . You're the lowest of the low now . . . I'm not okay with what you've done to me . . ."

"I'll kill you!"

"Go ahead. I'm waiting. I have nothing left to lose. You're already hit rock bottom. I'm there with you, unfortunately for me. Might as well end it here, right now. You want to drag me with you through this life that you think is free, but I don't want that. Come on, then. Kill me. Kill us. Come on. Come on. Are you scared?"

"I love you!"

"What? What did you say? You've gone insane, apparently."

"I love you!"

"Bullshit! You're killing me, you're cutting me off, you're erasing my existence, and you tell me that you love me . . . Yeah right, Zannouba! Yeah right!"

"It's true, I love you. You're just a little boy. It has nothing to do with you, this tragedy. It's not your fault at all."

"I don't understand these mysterious words."

"You know what I'm talking about. Don't play games with me, Aziz . . . Please . . ."

"I'm not playing. I'm not Aziz anymore. You killed me. You removed me from you. From your body. I'm nothing. Where should I go now? I'm in a situation worse than yours. I no longer exist. You, at least, can play the depressed, crying diva. You exterminated me. You have no pity for me. You don't think of anyone but yourself. Become a woman.

Become a woman. Now that you are one, you should be elated. You should believe in Allah again. Do it. Do it. He is the one who allowed this to happen. But, of course, narcissistic as you've always been, you think only of your own trivial unhappiness, your small negligible scars, your lost rhythm. And me? ME, AZIZ? Do you still think of me? Of course not. You're too busy becoming a madame. A madame like all those floozies hanging around this shitty city! Is that life, the future, emancipation? Becoming like the others around here? Is that it? Answer me! Say something. Look at me. Look at me and tell me you regret it . . . Say it . . . Say it . . ."

"No. I can't say it."

"You're heartless. You're letting me die. And you're crying over yourself."

"You don't understand, Aziz."

"Of course I don't understand, since I'm dead. By your hand, dead. By your hand, executed. Do you still remember, the crime you committed just two months ago?"

"It wasn't a crime. I had to find peace."

"I'm happy for you, Zannouba. I see how much good this peace has done you."

"Don't joke . . . Don't joke, please . . ."

"I'm not anything anymore. Not a little boy dancing happily with his sisters, nor a free soul still blissfully ignorant. You destroyed everything with your crazy desire to become a woman. You finished me. You ended all my opportunities, on earth and up above . . ."

"You will always be a part of me, Aziz."

"You're deluding yourself, Zannouba. Soon you will

even have forgotten my name. Our name. Aziz. You'll trample me, my heart, my cock. Now all you see is you: woman. The traces of us, little boy, man, are still here, in you. But rest assured, they will soon disappear. From where I am, from where I'm speaking to you, I see your future. I cursed you as a man. I cursed you as a woman. And, despite myself, I will continue to watch over you . . . Goodbye . . . Goodbye, Zannouba . . ."

"No, Aziz . . . No . . . Don't go . . . Stay a little longer."

"To do what? Let me go somewhere else, find another life to cohabit. Let me leave you. Don't argue . . . Set me free . . ."

"Do you remember Isabelle Adjani?"

"Yes. As a little boy, I used to adore that actress."

"Then you forgot about her."

"What are you getting at, Zannouba?"

"Before leaving for good, before abandoning me, let me tell you the story of Isabelle Adjani."

"Tell me what about her? I don't understand."

"Do you want to hear? . . . Do you, Aziz? . . ."

"Go on! Do your Scheherazade thing, Zannouba . . . I don't have a lot of time but I'm listening."

ISABELLE ADJANI

She is Algerian like you and me.

She appears. She disappears. She reappears. She is here. She is no longer here. We search for her. We thought we had forgotten her. But she is always somewhere. She hides. She sleeps. She forgets herself. She loves. She goes far. Very far. I think she frequently leaves this world, what we call the world: the round earth, the blue and black sky.

I'm convinced: Isabelle Adjani is not like the rest of us. She is not made of flesh and blood. There is only water in her body. This woman carries in her something we don't know yet. The future? The future as it's depicted in science fiction movies? Better. Much better than that. Man and woman reunited in another time. Not the present. Not the past. But what will come, that sublime explosion that never stops expanding and whose first echo we sometimes hear at night.

Isabelle Adjani was born then, in that moment. Precisely. I think we call it the Big Bang. There was nothing. Absolutely nothing. *Booommm!* Everything begins. Life. Not life as we know it today. No. Life in a mad rhythm, a hellish but completely bearable heat. A cosmic conscience. There are not yet human beings, other beings, other creatures, other intelligences. But Isabelle Adjani. So white. So black. So blue. Nude, of course. Carrying in her all the lives. Speaking all the languages. Mastering all the signs.

She is not a goddess. She is the spark. Her fire captured us. Humankind is forever attached to her. In fear. In ecstasy. We listen through her. We hear what happens in her. The voices of All the World. We exist to follow her, love her, adore her, venerate her. Wait for her.

Is she coming? Is she here? Not yet? Not yet.

In fact, she is already here. In us. In you. In me.

This world, today, doesn't understand Isabelle Adjani. Doesn't love her the way she deserves. Men see her only as a very talented and very temperamental actress. They're wrong. Ten thousand times wrong. Isabelle Adjani, the actress, cannot be defined by the idea of a career. She is beyond that, that modern triviality. To say that she is making a career is an insult to someone like her. That woman invents and acts out things that are much more modern than we could imagine. Incarnations and interpretations that tell us everything. Absolutely everything.

Do you understand, Aziz? Are you following me? I know that you love Isabelle Adjani just as I do. Remember how the two of us were swept away by *The Story of Adèle H*? Do you remember that movie? We watched it one sad afternoon on Algerian television.

Do you remember what she says near the end?

"That unbelievable thing, for a young girl to walk on water, cross from the ancient to the new world to join her lover, that thing will I do."

That's what she said, isn't it? She's the one who said it, not the character.

It's possible I've mixed up her words. It doesn't matter. Those words convinced us that this woman was indeed from our home country, Algeria in shambles, and also from the other world. Her conviction and her fervor sent unforgettable shivers down our spines, gave us memories that would last forever.

You and I tried to learn by heart the sacred words she spoke in the film. We might have invented them, reinvented them.

The film entered, once and for all, into our eternal memory.

The face of Isabelle Adjani who loves. Who suffers. Who

cries. Who yells. Who runs. Who jumps. Who falls. A haunted face, inhabited by all of us. One face and only one face. And nothing else.

We never grew tired of it, did we, that dear and tortured face, madly in love, courageous and alone, in writing, in clairvoyance, in the beyond.

Isabelle Adjani is also a clairvoyant. In the proper sense of the term. She sees. Here. Beyond. The man who made this film truly understood her. He placed Adjani in situations where the world ceases to be the world. The world ends. Adjani continues.

For weeks and weeks, every day we cried thinking about that film, that body in love, that wandering, that distress, that sadness, that absolute solitude, embraced.

And when we learned that this woman was Algerian, do you remember what we did, Aziz?

We went to the hammam.

You went to the hammam, Aziz, and you tenderly made love with three men at the same time. That was your way of being in love and in recognition. You understood then the reason for that mysterious and miraculous attachment to Isabelle Adjani.

She was better than Algerian. Within her flowed something that you too had, and that you recognized so clearly in her.

You weren't wrong. No. No. Adjani was from another world. Yours. You saw in her your idea of possession: how one takes within oneself the entire universe, before and after, how one adorns oneself in it, how one dances and cries in it.

Isabelle Adjani was exactly that: the truth according to

you. Beauty as seen through your eyes gazing at the world, and what they had captured, stolen.

You know why I wanted to come to Paris so badly? You know why Zahira is my only sister in France?

Like us, she worships Isabelle Adjani. Like us, she believes only in her.

Zahira said: "Isabelle Adjani is a saint." I can't help but agree with her. And you do, too, I know. Saints are neither pure nor chaste nor kind. They have needs. Zahira and I, we have honored Isabelle Adjani countless times. Several *Lila*. Several magical Nights.

An entire night to satisfy those who inhabit the body of that woman, those who inhabit us. Whether they be jinns, spirits, the living dead, the wounded lovers, fathers and mothers on another voyage.

We closed the windows to Zahira's studio. We burned rare incense. We wore green caftans. And we started to watch a film. The Film. *Possession*. Isabelle Adjani speaks English in it. In cold, foreign places, far from us, but because she was in the very heart of these places, we accepted those images and we awaited the moment. The Moment. Something unique. Never before seen, in the cinema or elsewhere.

Adjani is in blue. Her skin is whiter than ever. Her lips are bloodied, incredibly red. She leaves the subway. The yellow train. She climbs the unending staircase. There is no one. The hallways of the subway station are no longer hallways. Zahira and I, we know what's going to happen. But we forget every time that we are the ones who have organized this ceremony.

Adjani doesn't act. That's her great strength. She is incapable of acting. She is. She is. We know that. We understand it. We take her hand. We are with her. In her. The world will soon fall into a trance. The superseding of every limit.

Adjani has freed herself from every burden. She outdoes herself. She overflows. She yells. She shouts. She laughs. She falls. She drags herself along the ground. She flows. She flutters. Levitates. Kneels. Turns her head as quickly as possible and in every direction.

She frees herself. She comes back to the center.

She waves her hands. The visible. The invisible. She is no longer named Isabelle nor Adjani.

Some people, faced with these images, might be afraid. Others would make fun. And still others would analyze them too intellectually. Zahira and I, we don't need to study what Adjani did. We are exactly like Isabelle Adjani, in the same state as her. We breathe in her gestures. We reenact her choreography.

We stop the film. We rewind. To the moment when she leaves the subway.

Play it again.

Zahira is standing in her studio. I'm next to her. Isabelle Adjani turns around. Towards us. She sees us. She welcomes us. We rush forward. We enter the screen. Our bodies are frantic. Already in recognition. We follow the path.

The fire is blue. Adjani, like the world, is its exact reflection. Through love, through submission, Zahira and I, we become blue. Us too. We fall under the eternal trance.

Do you remember all this, Aziz? No? Were you still with me then? Or had you already planned your voluntary departure, even before I made the appointment with Dr. Johansson?

No answer?

Where are you?

Don't leave me alone, Aziz. I just arrived in this new world of women. Don't leave, please. It's too soon. You are my heart, my shadow, my secret soul. My past still flowing through my veins. Don't leave.

Are you coming back, Aziz? Are you listening, Aziz? What am I going to do without you? Where do I go? What direction do I take? Zahira, again? Zahira, always? Come back . . . Come back . . . Aziz . . . Aziz . . . Aziz . . . Don't leave . . . Don't leave me. Paris has turned cold, unresponsive, sad, indifferent. Racist. Paris will kill me. I need you. The little hand of a carefree boy who dances and sings. I need your forever-free soul. I need it.

Come back. Come back. Come back.

Don't die, my little brother. Come back. Paris is a black hole. Come back and save me. Come back and love me, wash me, carry me to my deepest desire, my last breath. Come back. I'm nothing without you.

Nothing.

2. Green Everywhere

MOJTABA. THAT'S HIS NAME.

He fled his country, Iran. A year ago.

He had always dreamed of going to France to visit the Jardin du Luxembourg. And to do so, he had to go to Paris.

Mojtaba wants to live in London or Stockholm. He doesn't know yet which of those two cities to choose. But he must make a final decision in a few days. Between now and the end of the month of Ramadan.

Mojtaba was lost near the Couronnes metro stop when I met him. He was standing at the station exit. He looked completely disoriented, in a huge panic. All around him, nothing but Arabs who had come to that neighborhood, the night before the beginning of the sacred month, to buy the necessary provisions: dates, dried fruit, honey cakes, little bottles of orange blossom water, special herbs, essences, oils, and countless other things. Like everyone else, I had also come to do some grocery shopping, pretend, convince myself for no reason that Ramadan in Paris had meaning, was worthwhile. I was lying to myself, of course. But by now it had been a long time since that bothered me.

I don't know why I walked towards Mojtaba. A need to do good? To save someone? Perhaps.

I planted myself in front of him. I looked at him. He lifted his eyes towards me. And then, I saw what he really looked like. In a word: he was sublime. A magnificent young man. And, clearly, lost.

I could tell right away that he wasn't Arab. Muslim, yes, but not Arab. He was also tender, sweet, melancholic. That was obvious immediately. Something in him was similar to me, familiar.

It wasn't love at first sight.

Compelled by some kind of fraternal sentiment, I moved towards him. I had no control over it.

His eyes were tired, his cheeks very hollow. He had a soft beard that asked to be caressed. His limbs were weary. He seemed to be beyond exhaustion. It was clear he was going to fall over, faint, any second now.

Mojtaba kept looking at me.

I grasped every part of his soul. I watched his destiny unfurl entirely in front of me.

He comes from far away, this boy, very far away. He's been wandering for a long time. He sets off. He moves around permanently. He no longer has a center. He no longer knows where to find the energy that will keep him alive.

I drew closer to him. I linked my arm through his. He needed it. He asked me a question, in broken, charming French:

"Is Barbès far?"

I answered with a big smile:

"Not really. A little farther on the 2 line."

He didn't have time to hear my response. He lost consciousness.

Outside of a moment of sexual ecstasy, I had never seen that before. A fainting man who loses control of his body, his mind, his energy. A falling man.

I fell with him, trying to hold him up, to slow the downward momentum of his body. I succeeded.

Now my butt was on the ground and the young man in my arms. People started to crowd around us. Normally indifferent, they were suddenly kind.

"What can we do to help, ma'am? Tell us . . . Tell us . . ."

I asked them to hail me a taxi.

Of course, as always in Paris, it was impossible to find one that was free.

After fifteen minutes, a woman passing by thought to call a car on her cell phone. She had the number for a service.

I've lived through a lot of dramas and tragedies in Paris. I've known the dirty, the rotten, the sordid, the unspeakable. Nothing surprises me anymore. Nothing affects me anymore. Only my mad love for Iqbal guides me, serves as my compass. I've seen it all. And I've survived it all.

In my entire life I had never witnessed anything more beautiful than that encounter with the boy from far away who fainted in my arms.

I didn't try to wake him up there. I just made sure he was still breathing, and brought his head to lie near my breasts. If I'd been able, I would have breast-fed him.

I know Parisians. And I know Arabs in Paris. They rarely help each other. Every man for himself. Everyone in his bubble. His cell. Especially in the streets. The metro. The buses.

Mojtaba inverted, reversed, that well-established order. At the moment when everything was going very badly, when the paths of our dishonest lives were leading nowhere, there was a moment of grace. Everyone ran over to save this young man who had fainted. Bring him back to life. Take his hand. Give him warmth.

"What's wrong with him, ma'am? What's happening to him? What can we do?"

"We can't let him die. He's so young. So handsome . . ."

"Put this small lump of sugar in his mouth!"

"Read a short sura from the Quran! Go on! Go on!"

I did it all. I followed their advice.

I cried. I wasn't the only one.

I prayed. I wasn't the only one to do that, either.

No one thought to ask me the indecent question of what was my relationship with Mojtaba. They must all have sensed, seen, the clear thread that connected us. Even the taxi driver was touched. He refused payment and helped me carry the young man into my apartment.

That night, I refused all my clients. I turned off my cell phone. And I watched over Mojtaba.

I heated up some milk with thyme. I poured it into a large bowl. I added a lot of sugar. And I made a date pastry.

I gave all of it to Mojtaba while he was still asleep. It took a lot of time. I opened his mouth and slid a spoonful of very sweet hot milk inside. I withdrew. And I started again.

I waited near his body for two hours.

I took off his jacket. His shoes. I covered him in a green floral sheet. Then I turned to his large traveling bag. I opened it. Took out his clothes. They were all dirty. I washed them by hand. I hung them all around the apartment to dry.

I took a white towel and dampened it with hot water. I took off Mojtaba's socks and, with the help of the hot towel, set about wiping and warming up his feet.

It was this heat that brought him back to the world. He opened his eyes. He looked at me. A bit shocked. I looked at him. He recognized me. He wasn't afraid. And he spoke, in a language I didn't understand. He began again, in hesitant French:

"Merci . . . Merci . . . Merci beaucoup. Je m'appelle Mojtaba."

I answered, with a softness that was new to me:

"Welcome to my home . . . I'm Zahira . . . I'm Moroccan . . . And you?"

He looked at me for a few long seconds.

"I'm Iranian."

I have to admit that I was a bit surprised. Before he revealed his nationality to me, I would absolutely not have guessed his home country.

Before I met him, I had never heard a first name like his. Mojtaba.

In a vague, intuitive way, I understood and invented a meaning for that word, for that Persian name. Something like "He who aspires to . . ." "He who answers to . . ." "He who moves towards . . ." "He who goes . . ."

Maybe I was wrong.

Mojtaba took his arm out from under the green sheet and extended his hand to me. I extended mine. Our hands met. Each shook the other. For a long time. No ambiguity. No malevolence. No false sentiment. Eventually I lowered my eyes. I had become timid again as though I were a pure little girl. I let go of his hand. I got up and went to the kitchen to prepare something for him to eat. His voice followed me. It asked me a question:

"Is tomorrow Ramazan in France?"

Ramazan! What was he talking about? After a few seconds, I finally understood that he was talking about Ramadan.

I turned back towards him.

"Yes, tomorrow is the beginning of Ramazan in Paris."

He asked another question, a bit disconcerting:

"Do you fast?"

His question told me that he did, he fasted. So I lied:

"Yes, I do."

Without hesitating, he proposed the following, this voyage through time:

"Let's fast together?"

I didn't hesitate.

"Okay, Mojtaba. We'll fast together . . . Okay . . ."

From a distance, I could see that he was smiling. I went back to preparing my dish and I too was smiling. I was delighted. Mojtaba would be staying with me for an entire month.

I refused clients during those first three days of Ramadan.

I had to find a way to make him understand the nature of my profession. Surely he noticed that, during the day, my cell phone almost never rang. At night, however, after the break of fast, the calls came nonstop. I never answered in front of him. I would go out on the landing and repeated the same lie to everyone: "Sorry, I'm really sick. Call back in a few days." And I would return to the apartment, where Mojtaba seemed to have made himself at home.

Nothing about him bothered me. Every day I liked his physical and spiritual presence a little bit more. His voice. His innocence mixed with a certain feeling of revolt.

Ramadan is of course an exhausting month. We would sleep in late every morning. In the early afternoon, we would watch Egyptian TV series on cable or else I would show him a few of my favorite Indian movies. Around six o'clock, I would prepare the abundant meal we ate to break the fast.

Without much effort, I taught him to love the food Moroccans eat during the month of Ramadan.

To begin: *harira*, crêpes with a mixture of honey and olive oil, scrambled eggs with cumin, hot milk with thyme, date purée.

Two hours later: very sweet mint tea with *sfouf* and different kinds of *chabbakiya*.

Late at night: a tagine.

I prepared all the secret tagine recipes I knew for Mojtaba. His favorite was the same as Zannouba's, the one with lamb, potatoes, fennel, candied lemon, and olives. It's the fennel flavor that changes everything, permeates everything. Zannouba told me one day that she had had a dream in which she was sharing that tagine with Zineb, my father's sister who disappeared several years ago. Zineb was happy, all smiles, and she was the one feeding Zannouba. When she had this dream, Zannouba was still going by Aziz and she had seen a sign in it: she absolutely had to fulfill her destiny, become a woman, entirely woman. Finally make an appointment with the surgeon to do the deed.

Zannouba gave a name to this dish: Zineb's Tagine. She insisted that Zineb had prepared the dish through me. That was how she visited us.

Mojtaba only stayed with me one month. He requested the fennel tagine at least twice a week. After watching me make it over and over, he eventually learned my recipe by heart.

"I will always remember this dish, Zahira. Always."

I know that he'll keep his promise. Whether he's in London or Stockholm now, I know that he makes this tagine from time to time. For himself. Only for himself.

At the end of the fifth day, Mojtaba started to go out for walks between ten o'clock and midnight. I managed to see all my clients in quick succession during those two hours.

When he returned, we ate. We watched Arab television channels and, sometimes, Iranian channels. I learned, thanks to him, that I could access those channels on cable, too.

Just before dawn, we drank hot milk, we ate a few dates, and got ready for bed. We brushed our teeth. We both lay down in a corner. We turned out the lights. Sometimes Mojtaba very softly sang the poems of his country. I didn't understand them. But I loved them. All of them.

I know nothing about Mojtaba. His life from before. His education. His parents. His loves. His future.

I see Mojtaba. I let him do as he pleases. He doesn't ask for anything. He just wants to stay with me.

I live through Mojtaba's life. His life, which he creates with me, in front of me. For me.

I give what I can to Mojtaba. Everything.

I'm the one who rubs his back when he washes himself, every two or three days, in my tiny shower. I don't turn away when he changes his clothes. I look. I look at that entire Iranian body, Persian with a hint of Muslim. Day after day, that naked body and its details worked their way into my memory. My heart.

An incredible sweetness. A sea of tenderness. Rivers of infinite love.

One day, almost at the end of Ramadan, he said to me:

"I've dreamed for a long time of going to the Jardin du Luxembourg. Do you know it?"

I was a bit taken aback. Apart from the Eiffel Tower, Sacré-Coeur, and Notre Dame, I wasn't really familiar with the Parisian monuments. And the idea of visiting them had never crossed my mind.

"By name, Mojtaba. Only by name."

Then he suggested:

"I want to visit it today, Zahira. Will you come with me? Is it far from here?"

It was very hot that day. We walked through the neighborhoods and the arrondissements that separated us from the garden.

Barbès. Gare du Nord. Gare de l'Est. Rue du Faubourg-Saint-Denis. Les Halles. Châtelet. Cité. Saint-Michel.

Odéon. Saint-Germain. Saint-Sulpice. Rue Servandoni. Jardin du Luxembourg.

Place Saint-Sulpice, he wanted to visit the church. I followed him. He showed me several paintings on the walls. He stopped for a long time in front of one of them. It was clear he knew it and had loved it for a long time. It was of a man and an angel fighting each other near a river and a tree. Who are they? Who will win? Their combat seems eternal. In that church, it had only just begun. Behind them, other men, probably traveling. Paying no attention to what's happening in the foreground. The dispute was taking place only for Mojtaba and me.

I left the church and waited on the steps. The sun was beating down hard. It triumphed.

When Mojtaba joined me, I suggested we go have a drink before entering the garden. That didn't shock him. Neither of us mentioned that it was still Ramadan.

We ordered the same thing. Orangina. Me first. He did the same. That quenched our thirst, refreshed us.

We didn't linger too long at the café.

It was nearly eight o'clock when we arrived at the Jardin du Luxembourg. There was only an hour before closing, and that night, that immense garden, imposing, grandiose, was already nearly empty.

Mojtaba looked at me. He was delighted.

"The French are gone. The garden is ours."

"Only for an hour, Mojtaba. Don't forget."

"That's fine."

"Let's stay together, Mojtaba?"

"Let's stay together, Zahira."

He took my hand and led me around to all the different monuments. He listed several things about the history of the site, its construction, its multiple renovations, its architecture. I remember nothing. It must not have interested me. He cited numerous complicated French names that didn't mean much to me, either. I quickly forgot them. Near the large pond, he let go of my hand.

"Wait for me here, Zahira?"

"Why?"

"Don't worry. I'll come back."

"But there's no one left in the garden, Mojtaba. They'll kick us out soon."

"I know. Don't worry. I'll be back in five minutes."

That garden was foreign territory. For five long seconds my body was shot through with monumental panic. I managed to stifle it without knowing where I drew the necessary energy to do so. I looked around me. What I saw was familiar. Grass. Flowers. Some trees. Then, no, no longer familiar. I had never come here, to this neighborhood, to this world. I had never breathed in this scent. I recognized certain buildings that are part of the history of this country, but only from distant memories. Old images of Paris glimpsed on Moroccan television, alongside my father sometime before his death. They were meant to inspire dreams. To crush us a little bit, too. *That world is not for you. Look, but only from a distance, through a screen. Don't come. Stay where you are. It's not for you.*

I must have received the message loud and clear because,

ever since I've lived in Paris, I've never had the desire to visit this garden, beautiful and cold. Mojtaba didn't have this feeling towards Paris. He was only passing through.

I understood his fascination for this city and its cultural riches, but we didn't share the same connection to it. That didn't have any bearing on the important thing: I was with Mojtaba, sharing a moment. Just for him.

I already felt the desire to return to my territory, my Paris.

I plunged my gaze into the pond before me. I saw phantoms within it. Not jinns. Ancient phantoms on the verge of emerging.

I closed my eyes immediately. The panic attack was returning. I cried out:

"Mojtaba! Mojtaba! MOJTABA!"

I opened my eyes. He was there. In front of me.

"Come, Zahira. I found it."

"You found what?"

"Don't talk. Follow me . . . Follow me . . ."

He took my hand again. And we hid ourselves in a dark corner.

The groundskeepers passed by.

Night fell.

In the Jardin du Luxembourg, there were now only two foreigners. Two freeloaders. Two children getting ready to start playing, or brawling, or chasing. A brother. A sister.

We didn't sleep that night. Mojtaba opened other doors for me. Other worlds. Other secrets.

The oppressive summer heat hadn't subsided.

When we were exhausted from walking through the garden in every direction, we collapsed onto the grass. Mojtaba took out sweets from his pockets and his backpack.

It was our meal to break the fast. And our dinner, too.

Then: sleep came.

The nocturnal noises of Paris ceased. Everything would now mix together. The barriers created by men would now cease to exist.

Return to the first world.

When I woke up early the next day, Mojtaba had disappeared. Forever.

Next to me, he had left two letters. In the one meant for me, he thanked me very warmly, bade me farewell, asked me to mail the second letter, and gave me permission to read it before sending it.

I left the garden, sad and angry.

I walked back through Paris the way I had come. I could have taken the metro. The desire to retrace the steps I had taken the day before with Mojtaba was stronger.

Next to a post office in Barbès, I found a Turkish translator who also spoke Farsi. His office was small, empty. He invited me to sit down. I preferred to remain standing while he translated the other letter for me.

MOJTABA'S SECOND LETTER

Dear Mama,

A warm hello to you and to your heart.

In this world I'm in, which you will probably never see, everything is new. Everything is already in motion. Decided forever. It's called Paris. The capital of France. You know, that country where my father's brother went to live after the revolution of 1979, and where he died, probably murdered, two years later. I am here. In this city. In this name, Paris, empty of meaning for you, quickly filling for me.

I'm only passing through. I met a woman. Her name is Zahira. She has a beautiful soul. She's put me up for almost a month now. I will leave her very soon. I don't dare tell her goodbye.

I don't know how to say goodbye.

I am going to entrust her with this letter that you are reading now. I told her that she could read it. It is written in Farsi. Zahira will find a translator so as to understand the words I've written to you. Through these words, my words for you, Mama, you two will meet.

Hello to you, Zahira.

Hello to you, Mama.

I don't know if you will see each other one day. Destiny and fate have carried me elsewhere.

I had to flee Iran and Tehran, Mama. I didn't have a choice. I hope that you'll answer: "Yes, I know, Mojtaba, I know."

They left me no choice. I had to save my life. Leave right away. Or else, prison forever. They were looking for me. The regime's assassins. The secret services wanted to end the 2009 revolution at any cost. Kill the youth and the massive protest. Put out the big fire. We didn't want that puppet president, Ahmadinejad, that man for whom the majority of Iranians hadn't voted. I was among the youth, Mama. I never told you that face-to-face. But you understood everything. And we remained silent. As always. I know that the silence between you and me is not like their silence. The silence that they impose on everyone from morning to night. In our house, there was no one but you and me. I thought of you, alone. But I never thought of the silence that surrounded you, too. How is it now, that silence? How are you, without me? How is Tehran in this moment, without the Green Movement, without the clamor of fury? Are you eating, Mama? Are you eating well? Are you sleeping? Are you sleeping well?

I know that you can read a bit of English. In the envelope containing this letter you will find photocopies of articles I wrote for the English press. I was a secret correspondent for the paper the Guardian. *Eventually they figured everything out. By finding me in the middle of the street, participating in the protests, too.*

They shot at me, Mama! I saw death! I saw death!

I had no choice. I had to leave.

I didn't want to implicate you in all of that. I didn't want them to find you. You have nothing to do with this. They must have paid you a visit after I fled. I'm sure of it. I hope that they didn't do you any harm. Mama, read these articles and then burn them immediately. Don't wait to do it. Follow this advice. It's very important. I don't want to scare you. I'll get out of this. I'll figure it out. I'll always find a solution. A place. A roof. A meal to eat. But I do want to tell you that I'm tired. So tired. It's been exactly a year since I was forced to leave. From one day to the next, I had to leave everything. Exit the world. That name: Iran. That life. I never wanted to leave Iran. I feel attached to everything over there. To everything that is you, us, that we created together. To everything that I inherited. I never wanted to turn my back on you. Abandon you. Flee. In any event, boys like me never leave their mother. I feel like I am in the void. Everything is empty. Even Paris is empty. They threw me over the highest edge. A year later, I'm still falling.

Still falling.

I wanted to tell you all of this, Mama. It's important. I am neither an angel nor a devil. I am neither a pious Muslim nor a washed-up drunk. But once, I dreamed, too. That's all.

For them, that's my crime. They say that I betrayed the nation, Islam, History, the people, the soul of the Iranian people, and I don't know what else. It's not true, Mama. Don't believe them. Don't believe them. Paris was only a stopover. I have the choice between London and Stockholm. I think they'll find me again pretty easily in London since they know everything. All I have left is Stockholm. I'll ask for political asylum over there. I'm sure that must sound like a very exciting possibility, Stockholm. Not for me, Mama. I have no idea what that city is really like, outside of books and certain movies. I have nothing against Stockholm. I don't see myself living there. I don't want to live in an idea, inside of a city-idea. Yet I must go there tomorrow. Without saying goodbye to Zahira. It's my destiny. To not know how to say goodbye. I was never able to find the courage within myself to do it. I don't know anything, or almost anything, about Zahira. She doesn't know anything about me, either. Through this letter, she will finally learn a bit about me.

Zahira: I know where you live, I have your email address, I will preserve within me the taste of you and your food. I will come back one day. We will see each other again. It's fate.

I'm on my way. Already in Stockholm perhaps. Already lost over there. As I write this letter, I ache all over. I feel as though all the maladies from my past are awakening inside me, in my body, even those I had forgotten a long time ago, in childhood. Mama, you must know them better than I do. My intestines most of all: they never leave me alone. I always had a problem with them. In the end I got used to it. But now, it's becoming more than a problem. The suffering is enormous and unrelenting. I no longer know what to do to relieve myself. The herbs you used to give me, Mama, I won't find them here, in this part of the world. Going to the bathroom has become hell. I'm in there for hours. I try to remember some of the things you used to do. I reenact them on myself. I massage my stomach, my chest, and my calves the same way you used to do. It does me good, calms me down. I forget my suffering, my furious stomach, for a few moments. But the pain never stays away for very long. It will always be like that. Something distant returns, no doubt the me from before, the forgotten me, me always there, me coming back to avenge myself no doubt.

Sorry, Mama, to speak to you like this, as in books. I'm able to understand, analyze all that happens to me, all that awaits me. But never does it help me tolerate the life that's coming for me. Wandering. That will be my life from now on. But don't worry, Mama. I will survive. I will carry you in me and I will survive.

I would like to ask you a small favor. Maybe I shouldn't, but I have no choice. You are the only person who can help me.

I'm a little ashamed.

You remember Samih, my friend from university? He would often come over to our house. You liked him a lot, I think. He has brown hair and green eyes. Very skinny. You would say to him all the time: "You're too skinny, my boy. Eat! Eat!"

He would smile every time. He didn't dare respond. Once, in my bedroom, he told me to thank you with all his heart for your care and tenderness towards him. It touched him, your maternal, generous gaze. I don't think I ever communicated those thanks to you.

I saw Samih every day. I was more than linked to him. Through my heart. Through my love.

Do you understand, Mama?

I know that you understand.

So there you have it: for the last three months, I've had no more news from him. He hasn't sent me any emails. I'm worried about him. I'm afraid for him. I fear they've discovered our secret, intimate link, and also his participation in my political investigations for the English newspaper.

Samih lives in Beryanak, close to a small 24/7 supermarket. His family's house is yellow. With three floors.

I would like for you to go to that house. For you to ring the doorbell and ask how he's doing. You will invent a story to justify to his family your arrival at their house and, most importantly, why you want to know how he's doing.

Is that too much for you, to have to go knock on the door of people you don't know and, on top of it, to lie?

Well then, tell the truth. Say my name. Tell my story. My departure from the country for political reasons. My flight. Tell of your sadness. Your solitude. That will touch them and earn their trust. And they will speak of him. Samih.

Mama, it's important that you do this. I need to know what's happened to him. Is he in good health? Alive? Dead? Hurt? And why did he stop writing to me?

If his mother tells you that he's in prison, pray for him and don't go visit him. If she refuses to talk to you, don't insist. Try to guess what she wants to tell you, but don't insist. Like you, she wants to protect what she holds most dear, most dominant in her heart.

And if a miracle occurs, if Samih is at the house, ask to see him. And when he is before you, look at him, kind, tender, beautiful. In him you will find a bit of me, maybe even a lot of me.

Tell him simply: "Mojtaba asked me to tell you hello, salam. *He hasn't forgotten you."*

Is it too much, all of this, for you, Mama? Yes? No? I am far from you and the distance makes me bold. But you are still my mother. You are now more than my mother.

It was just us two in Iran. We couldn't count on anyone else.

Now, you are over there, separated from me, always, forever, a large presence within me.

I am here, in this empty world, without your prayers and without your anger.

You have to go see Samih's family. It will do you good. You will get out. You will walk in the streets. You will have a purpose. A mission. A bus to take. An address to look up. A yellow house to find. You will ring the doorbell. It might be Samih who opens the door for you. He will recognize you. You will recognize him.

Do it. Complete this step, this visit, Mama. Don't cry. No matter what happens, don't cry. Just close your eyes.

Go back to the house. To our home. It will still be daylight. You'll have to close all the blinds and draw all the curtains. You'll know where to go. To the center of our house. I will be there. I will be there. I am with you. No matter what happens after the visit to see Samih.

Allah cannot belong only to them. Zahira, the woman in Paris, knows him better than them. For me, because she believes in him, she will go to paradise after her death. Like you, Mama. With you. Samih and I: probably not. But that's okay. What matters: this note that I am writing to you from my own darkness.

You are not here before me. But I see you. I am not there, near you. But you see me? Right? Right?

See you soon, Mama. Very soon. You know where to write to me from now on. The secret address in Paris.

See you soon, Zahira. From the bottom of my heart, I say to you again: thank you, thank you, thank you.

We'll find each other again. All of us. One day. I am sure of it.

I'm sending tender kisses to you both . . .

Mojtaba
Paris, August 2010

3. May She Burn

SHE MUST DIE.

It's her destiny. That's the way it is. Useless to resist. It's stronger than all of us.

I am in your dream, Zahira. You can't do anything. I've taken control of everything in you. Do you hear me? I am in your head. In your night. Whether you like it or not, the race has begun. I can't stop anymore. Like so many others before me, I have received the order. Now I must execute it. I am in full pursuit. I'll admit that I didn't expect it at all. I didn't know that Masters and jinns were interested in men, too. They possess me now.

A force compels me. I've left everything. I walk. I run. I fly. Towards you.

The *mektoub* will be fulfilled, Zahira. Your *mektoub*.

You thought you had fled our world, our Morocco and its routine violence. You thought you were free forevermore. Far from all judgment, rid of us. Like your father's sister, Zineb, master of yourself. That you could leave and never come back. Zahira master of yourself. You thought you were capable of building the foundation of a new world somewhere else. Far from us. Far from our eyes.

You are who you are. Zahira, daughter of Salé, even in Paris. Sooner or later you'll have to come back to us. Dead or alive. From the beginning, your flight was cursed. Your aunt Zineb might have managed to forge another destiny for herself, to completely forget her origins, the voices of her childhood. Not you. You hear me? Not you. You are not Zineb. You will not be a legend like Zineb. No. No.

I had stopped thinking about you. I had almost completely forgotten our past. Your brothers came to see me twice a year. They made sure I was doing good work for you all, for you. Guard and tend to the land, your acres in Tadla, at the foot of the Atlas Mountains.

Your lands. The void. Two mountains over there. The sky that keeps on expanding. My shed. That was the scenery of my life after you.

I have to be here. Always here. Faithful guardian. Absolutely not leave this land. Surveying the threat that will never arrive. Today I know. Here. In the countryside, its heavy sadness and its routine crime. Here. The terrifying world and me. Alone. The wind that passes, blows without ever growing tired.

I've always done my work well. I bury my salary, two thousand dirhams per month, beneath my shed. Under me. The workers from a nearby factory would bring me something to eat every week. I paid them what was owed. They didn't speak.

One day, exactly one week ago, one of them said:

"Zahira is a whore."

Was he talking about you?

"Zahira, the girl you knew a long time ago, became a whore in France. In Paris."

Was he really serious?

"It's Zahira who pays for all of this here . . . And for you, too . . . She's the one who bought the land . . . Her parents got out of poverty thanks to her, thanks to her *haram* money . . . Even your salary . . ."

Silence. He lowered his eyes.

"Apparently your salary, she's the one who sends it every month, through Western Union."

I lowered my eyes. When I looked up again, the worker was gone. Had he really come to see me? Had he really said what he'd said? I was dreaming. Yes? No?

She must die.

It's her destiny. It is what it is.

I left the land, the shed.

I went to the souk. I searched for the worker for a long time, an entire day. I finally found him in the makeshift bar of the souk. He was drunk. But I needed to know the truth. It was the right time. So I slapped him, shoved him, knocked him to the ground. I threw myself on top of him. And I stared at him hatefully straight in the eyes. He admitted everything, a second time, in front of everyone:

"Yes, she's a whore, your Zahira. She opens her legs for infidels from morning to night. What she earns is what you earn. Sinful money . . ."

And he burst into laughter.

"Do you still want to marry her, Allal? Make her the mother of your children?"

That old dream had vanished from my heart a long time ago. Zahira no longer existed in me. Doesn't exist. Can no longer exist.

I broke two empty bottles of wine on the worker's head. He lost consciousness. His friends took care of him.

I got up. I left the souk. No one tried to stop me.

I returned to my shed. Far from everything, once again. I didn't sleep for three nights. At the beginning of the fourth night, I received my orders.

I saw them and didn't see them. But they were there, the Masters, in the darkness of my heart. They told me what to do. I am thrilled to obey. Everything must end. I have to see it through.

How could you do this to me, Zahira? Forget me completely and, years later, once more humiliate me, crush me, turn me into a faceless man? From far in the past, you returned to destroy what remained of my dignity. From over there, from the land of the French, you showed me your unabashed contempt once more. Your second and mortal vengeance.

For all those years, while everything in me was slowly forgetting you, you were the one paying me, without my knowledge. And even the land I was surviving off of, it belonged to you.

No. No. No. No. No! I cannot accept that. I don't want to fall all over again. I don't want your love or your pity, and even less your dirty money that you make with infidels.

I don't want to go back. To before you became a whore. Face your parents, who lowered their eyes rather than answer me.

They said nothing. Nothing.

"I want to marry Zahira. I want to make her my wife before Allah and his prophet Mohammed. I am in love with her. I think she loves me, too. I'm a nice man. As a mason, I earn a good living. I can rent and furnish an apartment not far from your house, for her and me."

Nothing. No response. I didn't let myself be discouraged. I fought to the end.

"She is your daughter. I will not steal her. I am a good person. I can work hard. I'm not afraid of hard work. I am a branch cut from a tree. I don't have a family. I have no one in the world. Zahira will be my world. Everything, absolutely everything, for me."

Nothing. Still nothing. And despair set in slowly.

Your mother finally looked up. Without saying a single word, she locked eyes with me. That told me everything.

Your father was no longer with us. He was leaving. He was slowly dying. Everyone in the neighborhood knew that he was very ill.

Finally, your mother gave me her categorical refusal:

"Go to the mirror, Allal, and look at yourself. You see who you are. Do you see? Do you understand? Zahira will never be yours. Not in this world, anyway."

Hiding in the kitchen, you heard everything, I know it, Zahira. Your mother, heartless, condemned me. Cut off my head and my feet.

You did nothing. You didn't cry. You didn't yell. You didn't even try to send me a discreet signal. Nothing. The void.

Already we weren't living in the same world anymore.

Later, I stood in front of the mirror. I looked, for a very long time. I saw what I am despite myself.

I am black. Moroccan and black. Moroccan, poor, and black.

You, you and your family, were Moroccans, poor, and not black.

Zahira must die.

It's her destiny. It is what it is.

I agree with that sentence. Death for her, too! Death by my own hand!

I am in full pursuit, Zahira. I will find you again easily in your Paris. There's no use hiding. Do you hear me? I am still in your head. I do what I want. I have the power now. They gave it to me.

You ask yourself: Who are they?

Don't play games, Zahira. You know them as well as I do. Your invisible Masters. Your jinns. They're mine now. I spent my whole life avoiding them, mollifying them. I didn't want to be possessed. I didn't want that. They conquered everything in my body, my heart, and my spirit.

I see through them. I travel through them. I'll have my vengeance thanks to them.

No pity for you, Zahira. I'll see this through. A man's life must have purpose. I've found mine.

For an entire year, you said to me over and over: "I love you, *khouya* Allal. You are my brother and my beloved. I love you. I love you. Take me . . . Take me far from here, from our sad reality . . . Take us . . ."

No one had ever said to me what you said to me. No one had ever so closely linked me to their dream of forever.

"I am yours, Allal, with or without their blessing. Take my hand. You have already stolen my heart. Take my right eye. My left leg. My thick lips. My overly large feet. Take everything. Everything. I am no longer me. I am yours. I am you. You, Allal, my love."

Why, Zahira? Why did you say all that to me? Why did you fill my head with those sweet, lofty words, straight out of Egyptian movies? Why?

Why, like a lamb that belonged to you, did you brand me for life? Who, now that you're gone, will help me navigate this narrow-minded world, leave it behind with no regrets? Who? How will I fly up high where it's beautiful, with you, kiss your wild and pure heart? Did you think of me, in an uncertain future, without your body to set me on fire?

Are you asleep, Zahira? Wake up. Wake up, Zahira, and tell me. Wake up and answer my questions. I'm giving you a chance to defend yourself. Go on! Speak! Explain yourself!

In front of the mirror, after the rejection from your mother, I repeated your words of love to hurt them, to hate them, to destroy them, to dishonor them.

Impossible.

I was screwed. Condemned to a life of suffering. Alone in suffering. Wretched despite myself. Over time I decided to remain in that state. In this cruel world, I had nowhere to go.

I didn't know Morocco. Your mother's eyes revealed its reality to me. The hatred. Profound. Blatant. Everywhere. Between everyone.

I'm nothing but a slave, is that it? A negro. An *azzi bambala*. The colored. The Touargui. An invisible. A less-than-a-man. Eternal servant. Eternal reject. I had no family. I thought I would belong to yours. To you. More or less. But, of course, there are lines one cannot cross. Even among the poorest of the poor, there are boundaries.

You are black. Black. BLACK. Don't ever forget it!

I so wish I had had the courage to pick myself up and spit in your mother's face. Throw that hatred and wretchedness right back at her, uncompromisingly and with no regret.

I wish I had cried out your name.

"Zahira! Zahira! Zahira, where are you? Come! Come save me! I'm sinking. I'm dying. They're killing me. Come. I don't want to be alone. Keep living alone. Zahira, my love! Zahira, my sister and my little girl! Zahira, my direction, my path! Zahira, my *quibla*! Zahira, my life and my end! All my most beautiful memories."

"I was born at night, you're right, little Zahira. How did you know? I was born the color of coal but I'm not bad, no. No. I was born far away."

"Where?"

"I'll never know."

That was our first conversation, Zahira. Our eyes met. I understood immediately. You understood, too, I know.

You were barely twelve years old. I was twenty-five.

We had to wait. Five years.

I never had any doubt. I knew nothing about you, about what was happening to you, about what was going on in your heart, your head. But you came. You didn't forget me.

You sought me out. You knew where to find me. You always ended up finding me. There were many construction sites at the time in Salé. I worked a great deal. And I earned a good life as a mason.

You would come and you would speak tenderly.

"I brought you crêpes with fermented butter. Do you like those, Allal?"

"I bought half a pound of mandarins for you, my brother Allal. Don't tell me you don't like this fruit."

"On my way back home, I passed a man selling candy apples. He gave me two but he only made me pay for one. It's for you, the second one. Take it, Allal . . . Take it, my brother . . ."

"Today my mother made an incredibly delicious dish with chickpeas and cow feet. You have to taste it, Allal. It's to die for. You'll see. I stole this piece for you. Go on, eat it! Eat it and tell me what you think."

"The bread is still hot, it's from the communal oven, Allal. I cut this piece and put a bit of olive oil on it. It's all we have these days at the house. It's not much. Do you want some? Take it. It'll give you some strength . . . Take it . . ."

Your mother is not a mother. Your heart, Zahira, though tender and generous, must possess some of that woman's hardness, her maliciousness. Her intransigence.

She scares me, your mother. She transforms men into statues, into sand, and she stomps all over them.

That day, faced with her death stare and her rejection when I asked for your hand, I was made to feel that I should never have been born.

I had to leave. Distance myself from your mother's anathema.

I fled.

Where to escape to when you know only one city in Morocco, Salé, only one river, the Bou Regreg, only one sea, the Atlantic Ocean?

Where to go to die a little bit more?

I left our neighborhood. Our Building 15. I escaped to the countryside. I crossed cities and medinas without ever stopping. Rabat. Temara. Mohammedia. Casablanca. Settat. Khouribga. El Ksiba. Souk Lakhmis.

I distanced myself from you as much as possible. I didn't want to recognize the air of the sea we had breathed together. I wanted to destroy the taste of life in me. Abandon myself to the wretchedness spreading everywhere.

Opposite the Atlas Mountains, I stopped. Not far from a city, Beni Mellal. But in the solitude of the countryside. Tadla.

That's where I let the years go by.

Oblivion exists. I sincerely wanted to believe that.

Your love had left. I don't know where it went.

My love: I smothered it with my own hands, night after night.

I went from being a mason to being a farmhand.

The Black Man. That's what they called me over there. I answered to it each time. What was the point of resisting? Might as well enter into that other skin. That negation.

"This life is only one life. Others will follow."

It was you, Zahira, who said that to me one day. Those obscure words.

I came to understand them and apply them in Tadla. In

the gradual oblivion of you. It was only the first life, I know that now.

I resigned myself. Elsewhere, I invented another hope.

One day, we will see each other again.

You're asleep, Zahira. You can't do anything. Destiny is on my side this time.

I know what I have to do.

You are in Paris, in France, in Europe. I am in Tadla, in Morocco, in Africa. Cities, seas, rivers, countries separate us.

Tonight, the borders no longer exist. I won't need a visa. I am beyond that now.

I've been preparing everything for a week. The big knife. Not Aïd el-Kebir's knife. An even bigger one. Two bunches of mint that I've dried. Two glasses of tea. Two pomegranates: your favorite fruit.

I sense your questions. I decipher them.

The knife is to slit your throat. The mint is to give you a taste of the other life. Paradise? One bunch in my right hand. The other in my left hand. The glasses: one to collect some of your blood, the other to break against your forehead.

The pomegranates: you know why. The symbol of love for an entire people, the Arabs, myself among them.

After completing the sacrifice, I will eat them both. Next to you, dead. I will take my time removing their seeds. Devouring them. And then, I'll drink some of your blood.

Complete the second sacrifice. Join you in your journey. In another land, another sky. Other colors.

This life is only one life. Others will follow. We both know that.

You will die. I will die. It's over.

Like your aunt Zineb, we will suddenly disappear. We won't leave bodies behind. For those who survive us, we will be a mystery. That will be their problem. They'll manage as best as they can to understand. Or not. Accept the unbelievable. Or not.

You have become impure. Dirty. Ruined. Deflowered from morning to night. I come, black, to kill you and bring you back to life. Avenge myself and resume my path with you there where your mother, with her cold eyes, put a stop to everything. I cling to this vengeance. I want to be a criminal for the men from here. May they have a terrible memory of me! May they say that I am in the end what they always thought I was! Savage. Bloodthirsty. A cannibal.

Yes, I am all of that. I am no longer afraid. Why be afraid? They are on my side now, the jinns, the Masters, the invisible world. Destiny tells me that I am right. I want to kill. I want to commit this crime. Spill human blood. That of the beloved. Of love. That or nothing. That or give up. It is out of the question to wait. I am leaving this very night.

It's midnight.

You're asleep, Zahira, over there in Paris.

In less than six hours I will be standing before you.

Your door is shut. Your body is destroyed. Your soul is lost. Through me you will be saved. Through me, through my vengeance, you will live for a long time. Through my crime, you will forget the rest. All the rest. You will change. You will turn black. Black like all of us.

Don't wake up. For the moment, I am still on this side.

Africa. Your origins despite yourself. Despite your tyrant mother and despite your sick father.

I won't get out of your head, Zahira. I am still in you. In love once more. A murderer on his way.

I see the Mediterranean Sea. With one step I cross it.

I reach Spain. In the blink of an eye I fly over it.

I'm in France. I climb. I climb. I climb. Biarritz. Bordeaux. Poitiers. Tours. Orléans. Paris. The Eiffel Tower. Dark streets. I know your studio. Your prison. I walk through the door. You're asleep. I am no longer just in your head and your dreams.

Open your eyes, Zahira. Open them!

You know me. Since our first life, you've known me. Yes, it's me. Allal.

Let it happen. Don't cry. Don't be afraid of this large knife.

It'll be easy.

It'll be fast.

Don't resist.

It's our destiny.

PART III
Indochina, Saigon, June 1954

I

"WHERE ARE WE, GABRIEL?"

"In my arms, Zineb."

"Don't make fun of me . . . I mean . . . in what country?"

"You don't know already? They didn't tell you when they brought you here?"

"Yes, yes, they told me. But they didn't explain anything to me. I don't know where we are exactly, where I am exactly. Where on this earth . . . But you must know . . ."

"I can draw the five continents on a piece of paper and show you where exactly . . ."

"No. Not like that. I'd rather you tell me with words . . . Where are we?"

"In my arms."

"I'm not kidding, Gabriel."

"We're in Indochina. Do you know that, Zineb?"

"Yes, yes. But what is Indochina? A country?"

"No, it's more like several countries, several regions in the south of Asia, that belong to France."

"You mean the way my country, Morocco, belongs to France?"

"Yes."

"Exactly the same way?"

"Yes."

"I see."

"As I said, this continent is called Asia . . ."

"Don't talk to me like a professor . . . Speak simply to me."

"Bordering us, not far from here, are Indonesia, China, Thailand . . ."

"The sea, does it have a name?"

"There are many seas all around, Zineb."

"Say their names, Gabriel . . . Say them . . ."

"All of them?"

"No. Just a few. I'll repeat them after you. Go on . . . Name them . . ."

"There's the Andaman Sea."

"The Andaman Sea."

"The Arafura Sea."

"The Arafura Sea."

"The Ceram Sea."

"The Ceram Sea."

"The Tasman Sea."

"The Tasman Sea."

"The Pacific Ocean."

"The Pacific Ocean."

"The Indian Ocean."

"The Indian Ocean . . . Is India close to here, Gabriel?"

"Yes, you could say that . . . You know India?"

"I love India."

"You've been before?"

"Of course not! I had never left Morocco before coming here. I only know India through those Indian movies I used to see at the theaters in Casablanca . . ."

"Really?"

"I immediately fell in love with the actors in those movies . . . Especially the actresses . . . So beautiful, so spiritual . . ."

"Like who?"

"You don't know them, I'm sure."

"Say their names anyway, Zineb."

"Chadia. Do you know Chadia?"

"Is she brunette or blond?"

"Don't be an idiot . . . They're all brunettes, the Indian actresses . . . Sort of like Moroccans . . . But they're less harsh than Moroccans . . . More open . . ."

"Who else?"

"Tabu?"

"Tabu. That's pretty."

"And there's Nargis. My favorite. There were two girls with me in the brothel, in Casablanca, who had the same name as her."

"Nargis . . . Nargis . . . That's pretty."

"It's more than pretty . . . It's incredibly beautiful."

"And why do you like Nargis more than the others?"

"I don't know . . . When I see her I recognize myself in her. But I am not her. Nargis is me in another life . . . Is India very far from here, Gabriel?"

"That depends on where you want to go in India. India is huge."

"Oh . . ."

"You didn't know?"

"I didn't know . . . How many days does it take to get there by boat?"

"I would say five days, maximum."

"Five days! That's not a lot . . . Will you take me there, Gabriel?"

"One day, Zineb."

"I'm serious."

"To bring you there, first I'd have to leave the French army."

"Would you do that for me, Gabriel?"

"I can't. I don't have the right."

"You'll have to desert, then . . ."

"Don't joke about that kind of thing, Zineb. France is at war in Indochina. That's why I came here."

"But you've told me several times that you're in love with me."

"Yes, I am, Zineb. I'm madly in love with you."

"Then act madly . . . Desert your country's army and let's go to India . . ."

"Pffft . . ."

"No response? Don't you love me, Gabriel?"

"But surely I can't be the only one who loves you here. Practically all the soldiers at the base are in love with you. Don't they tell you that when they visit you for . . . for . . .?"

"The others just come for sex. Nothing more. That's why they brought me here from Morocco. Some of the French soldiers don't like the Asian women . . ."

"How do you know that?"

"Don't change the subject, Gabriel."

"Don't be so serious, Zineb. It doesn't suit you."

"Do you love me? Yes? No?"

"I love you, Zineb. You know perfectly well I do."

"Are you satisfied when I give myself to you each day, from the front and from behind?"

"Zineb, don't talk like that."

"I'm not ashamed of anything. I own it."

"Even so . . ."

"And when I tend to your cock and everything else, are you happy?"

"I am always happy with you, Zineb."

"Then bring me to India!"

"Even if I wanted to, the French army would never let me leave with you. You belong to them, Zineb. You work for them."

"I don't belong to anyone. I came here of my own free will. I whore myself out for these French soldiers because . . ."

"You're not a whore, Zineb . . ."

"Yes I am. You share me with the other soldiers, and you've never said that it bothers you. I give to them what I give to you. I spread my legs . . ."

"Don't talk like that."

"Do you tell them what I do with you? Do they tell you what I do with them?"

"What's wrong with you? Calm down. Calm down . . ."

"Do they tell you everything? Absolutely everything?"

"Zineb, that's enough . . . Be quiet . . ."

"Gabriel, if you love me, you'll take me to India."

"That's pure insanity."

"Yes, I'm insane. That's what you love about me. Isn't it?"

"Yes, that too . . . Your tendency to be . . ."

"Especially that, the insanity in me that I give to you. The sounds I make when we're having sex . . . It drives you mad . . . You told me all this, didn't you?"

"Zineb . . . Stop . . . Stop . . ."

"Why are you denying me the right to dream about India?"

"You're out of your mind."

"India belongs to France, too, right?"

"India belonged to England. Now it's a free country."

"India is a free country! Since when?"

"Seven years ago, I think."

"You see, it's simple, Gabriel. We'll go live in a free country. No one will arrest us over there."

"And Morocco? You can forget about it just like that, so easily?"

"Morocco?"

"Yes, Morocco."

"What has Morocco done for me?"

"That's for you to tell me."

"Nothing."

"Don't exaggerate."

"Morocco sold me to France, to the French."

"I don't understand."

"I didn't want to become a whore, you know . . ."

"I . . . suppose . . . that . . . no one wants . . ."

"Yeah? You suppose what? Finish your sentence."

"Nothing."

"You think I was born a whore? That I always lived in Bousbir?"

"You mean Prosper, I imagine."

"In Casablanca, we pronounce it Bousbir. It's simpler."

"Bousbir is a brothel in Casablanca?"

"Better than that. It's an open-air whorehouse. Where all the damned of Morocco end up, men and women alike."

"And everyone prostitutes themselves there?"

"Everyone. Well, as long as you're still a viable commodity."

"Is it big?"

"Several houses. Several streets. An entire neighborhood across from the sea, the Atlantic Ocean."

"They forced you to work over there?"

"It's more complicated than that."

"Go on, then . . ."

"Where to start? . . . It's difficult. It's a very long story."

"I'm your last soldier of the day. We have the entire night to ourselves."

"No. Not tonight. Tomorrow. I don't have the energy to rehash all of that tonight. Tomorrow."

2

"I WAS HIGH UP, in the Atlas Mountains, with my father and a Jewish sorcerer. We were looking for one of the treasures that had been buried there for several centuries. It was night. And this time, the Jew hadn't been lying. In a bewitching voice, he recited psalms, incantations, calls, both in Hebrew and in Berber. My father dug for more than two hours. The Jew continued his rituals. I helped my father as much as I could. I removed the earth from the sides of the deep hole. Suddenly, as in tales, a yellow, golden light appeared at the very bottom. Suddenly, the Jew stopped chanting. My father cried out. I went over to him and helped him pull out a sack containing at least twenty pounds of louis. Real louis from way back when. So beautiful. So heavy . . . I hope you believe me, Gabriel. I'm not telling you lies."

"I believe you, Zineb."

"Those stories of hidden treasures are really true."

"I believe you. Really. Continue. What happened next?"

"We divided up the twenty pounds of louis into three

baskets. We put dates on top of them and started to descend the mountain back to our village, which wasn't far from the city, Azilal. It took a long time. We got lost several times. In the early morning, we were stopped. The French police. More precisely, Moroccans who were working with the French. Someone had informed on us. I tried to resist, to yell. My father threw me a look. I gave up. They separated us. That was the last time I saw my father and the Jewish sorcerer . . . I was sixteen years old . . ."

"And after that?"

"I became what you see before you. Another woman."

"Were you in prison? Did they sentence you in court?"

"They took me far away, very far away from home. To another city. Marrakech. That's where I was supposed to be sentenced. But that didn't happen."

"They let you go?"

"The chief of police took pity on me. He got me out of prison. He said that I was young and surely didn't know what I was doing. And so they couldn't consider me an accomplice. I could go back home. I was so happy, so relieved. I got down on my knees and I kissed his feet, one after the other. He let me. Then he lifted me up, looked me straight in the eyes, and told me his name was Charles. And he added: 'Before you go back home, come to my house. You can rest for a bit. You'll work a bit. You'll earn some money, too. That way you won't go back to your family empty-handed.' He was kind, Charles. Very kind. From the first night, he proved it to me. He got into bed with me and slept on me . . . On me . . . Do you understand? Do you understand?"

"Yes."

"He was kind. He knew what he was doing. What he was condemning me to . . . The consequences . . ."

"What were they?"

"I was dishonored."

"That's bad."

"Very bad. Where could I go in that state? No one in my family would help me. I knew that perfectly well. So I stayed with Charles. I got used to him. I had no choice. He would say: 'You're so white, Zineb, and your hair is so black. I'm in love with you!'"

"You are not very white."

"I was at the time. It was the Marrakech sun that bronzed me."

"And after that?"

"Charles was promoted. They sent him to work in Casablanca. He brought me with him."

"What did you do for him?"

"Cooked sometimes. Mostly, I made sure his house was well maintained."

"That's all?"

"And had sex with him, of course. Every night."

"Every night?"

"He would tell me all the time that he was in love with me."

"And you, Zineb?"

"Me? I had no other choice but to stay with him."

"You wanted to stay with that man?"

"You don't understand, Gabriel. For a Moroccan woman in my circumstances, it was a perfect solution."

"Did you like Casablanca? Did you stay with him a long time?"

"One day, he told me he was going back to France. They were summoning him back there. He would end his career in Paris."

"And you?"

"He told me he would introduce me to one of his friends. His name was Augustin. An important functionary. 'You'll like him a lot, you'll see.'"

"And he gave you to him?"

"What do you think? Of course!"

"And you lived with Augustin?"

"One week. Just one week."

"You fled?"

"Yes."

"Where to?"

"I went to the bus station in Casablanca to take the bus to the mountains, to my home. The village next to Azilal."

"Azilal? After all those years?"

"But at the last minute, I changed my mind. It was impossible. Impossible. I couldn't go back like that."

"Why not?"

"They would have killed me, my parents . . ."

"Oh!"

"An older woman approached me in the waiting room of the bus station. She's the one who brought me to the Bousbir brothel . . . That's the end . . ."

"'That's the end'?"

"I stayed in Bousbir for two years. I was practically dead over there. From time to time, I went to the movie theaters in downtown Casablanca. That's where I discovered the actress Nargis and started to dream of her. Of becoming like her."

"I see."

"One day, I heard people talking about those Moroccan prostitutes who accompanied the French soldiers to the war in Indochina. I went to the prefecture and told them that I wanted to enlist for France, too."

"You weren't afraid?"

"Once you've lived in Bousbir, you're not afraid of anything anymore . . . And I felt I was being called. I had to go farther, distance myself from Morocco. Somewhere else, another destiny awaited me. Another life."

"And you hoped to achieve that dream by following the French soldiers to the war in Indochina?"

"It was the only solution I had."

"But it must be hard, even so, to sleep with all these soldiers every day."

"I never said it wasn't."

"And now?"

"Now I must continue my path. With or without you, I have to get to India. Nargis's country."

"Even if we manage to flee, the French army will catch us again. And our punishment will be terrible."

"You don't want to go with me. I get it . . . My story didn't move you."

"It's a big risk, Zineb. I'm French. I would lose everything by fleeing with you. Absolutely everything."

"But you said you were in love with me . . ."

"I am. I swear to you."

"I don't understand, Gabriel."

"What?"

"Do you really love me, or you just love me like that first French guy, Charles?"

"Don't compare me to him."

"We have one life. Why give yours to the war? For what?"

"For France."

"I've renounced Morocco."

"And? . . ."

"You could renounce France."

"It's not that simple."

"Actually, it's very simple. You come. Or you don't come."

"You're being harsh, Zineb."

"Don't be a coward, Gabriel."

"I love you, Zineb. Really. But . . ."

3

"I HAVE A DREAM. I know in my gut that it's real."

"What exactly is this dream?"

"To become like Nargis. To become Nargis."

"An Indian movie star."

"No. An actress."

"But you don't know how to act."

"How do you know? You think being a whore is my true nature, my true role in life?"

"I don't understand, Zineb."

"And yet it's quite simple. Being a whore isn't just taking your clothes off and opening your legs for men. You have to act out multiple roles, act them out perfectly in real life. Act and direct clients . . . I know everything about this profession . . . When I first saw Nargis in the movie *Andaz*, I understood all of it. I too can do what she does in front of the camera. Inhabit the film. The images. Be in the spotlight. Position myself as necessary in that light. Forget the others. Let another life penetrate me, come from me, from everything that is me. It seemed obvious to me . . . That's all acting is . . . I have to go there, to India."

"But why not try to become an actress in Morocco?"

"There's no film industry in Morocco."

"What about Egypt?"

"For me, it's India. India or nothing. I want to be in that dream, in a country where no one will stop me, remind me of my past as a prostitute. Not the Moroccans, not the French. I want to go directly into the light, without an intermediary."

"You're crazy."

"Don't make fun."

"You're crazy."

"Okay then, yes, I am. And all the better. Since delving into the images of the movie *Andaz*, I've gone crazy. I'll admit it. But that's the only thing that can really save me."

"What is that movie about, *Andaz*?"

"A woman who loves two men."

"I see. A liberated woman."

"No, actually. One cannot be liberated when one is equally in love with two men. For me, in that movie, that's not where liberty resides."

"Where is it, then?"

"In Nargis's acting. Her way of being an actress. She abandons herself. She abandons herself and she offers up all of her energy, all of her true colors. All of her secrets."

"Do you know what that's like?"

"Enough questions, Gabriel. Make a decision. Right now . . . Are you coming with me to India?"

"I have to give an answer right now?"

"Not a definitive answer, if you want . . . Just tell me that you'll come with me . . . That we'll go together . . ."

"I'll go with you, Zineb."

"Oh!"

"Are you surprised?"

"You really love me . . ."

"I don't want to die in Indochina."

"You want to live, like me. That's great, Gabriel. I'm glad. I'm happy. I can sleep."

"Sing first, Zineb. Sing."

"I'll sing 'Uthaye Ja Unke Sitam' for you, a song from *Andaz*. Nargis doesn't sing it. She pretends. It's Lata Mangeshkar who sings it."

"Lata Mangeshkar . . . How do you know her name?"

"When you look, you find."

"Go on, sing . . . Sing, Zineb . . ."

"Here I go:

"Uthaye ja unke sitam aur jiye jaa

Yunhi muskuraye ja, aansoo piye ja
Uthaye ja unke sitam aur jiye jaa
Yunhi muskuraye ja, aansoo piye ja
Uthaye ja unke sitam

Yehi hain mohabbat ka dastoor aye dil
Dastoor aye dil
Woh ghum de tujhe tu duaye diye ja
Uthaye ja unke sitam

Kabhi woh nazar jo samayi thi dil me
Samayi thi dil me

Usi ek nazar ka sahara liye ja
Uthaye ja unke sitam

Sataye zamana o, sitam dhaye duniya
Sitam dhaye duniya
Magar kisi ki tammana kiye ja

Uthaye ja unke sitam aur jiye jaa
Yunhi muskuraye ja, aansoo piye ja
Uthaye ja unke sitam."

"It's sad."

"Yes, very sad, Gabriel."

"You want to go to India so you can sing this kind of song?"

"Going to India, answering that call, will mean finally starting my life. My real life. Everything that has preceded that moment will have been only a step or two. Nothing more."

"And once I'm over there with you, what will I do?"

"You are my love. You will be my man. We will live together."

"We'll be in your dream only."

"My dream, yes, but you will discover yours, too . . . Soon . . . Along the way . . ."

"Where did you learn to talk like that?"

"Are you saying that I speak well?"

"Yes."

"The first French guy, Charles, didn't take me with him to Paris. He abandoned me. He didn't know, but I would watch him when he welcomed people to his house. He put himself center stage and, without shutting up the others, he would start to talk. To shine. To become someone else . . . I kind of stole that talent from him . . ."

"I get the impression you're not real, Zineb."

"You're not real, either, Gabriel . . . Being a soldier, that's not real . . ."

"What do you mean by that?"

"You don't seem to be affected by what you've seen, what you do . . . The horror . . . All the dead . . ."

"When are we going to India?"

"Come into my arms, Gabriel."

"Here I am . . . Where are we now, Zineb?"

"On the boat."

"And am I still in your arms?"

"Still."

"Can I close my eyes?"

"Yes. Yes, Gabriel. I'll wake you up when we're there. In five days."

"Will you go by the same name in India?"

"No."

"I'm not surprised. You've thought of everything. Even of all the ways to make me fall madly in love with you. That way you'll be able to do with me what you like."

"It's for your own good, Gabriel . . . Sleep . . . Sleep . . ."

"I'm drifting. I'm getting sleepy . . . Sleepy . . . more and more . . ."

"Sleep, my little Gabriel."

"What will your name be in India?"

"Zahira."

"Zahira . . . Why?"

"It sounds good."

"Yes. Zahira . . . That's beautiful . . ."

"A beautiful name for an actress in India."

"It sounds Arab."

"Nargis is an Arab name, too. It's her stage name. Her real name is Fatima Rashid. She's Muslim."

"Like you, Zineb."

"Like me, Gabriel."

Born in Rabat, Morocco in 1973, ABDELLAH TAÏA has
written many novels, including *Salvation Army*, which he
also made into an award-winning film, and *Infidels* (Seven
Stories 2016), translated by Alison L. Strayer. He lives in
Paris.

Translator EMMA RAMADAN is based in Providence, Rhode Island, where she co-owns Riffraff Bookstore and Bar. She's the recipient of an NEA fellowship, a Fulbright grant, and the 2018 Albertine Prize for Anne Garréta's *Not One Day*. Her other translations include Anne Garréta's *Sphinx*, Virginie Despentes's *Pretty Things*, Ahmed Bouanani's *The Shutters*, and Marcus Malte's *The Boy*.

SEVEN STORIES PRESS is an independent book publisher based in New York City. We publish works of the imagination by such writers as Nelson Algren, Russell Banks, Octavia E. Butler, Ani DiFranco, Assia Djebar, Ariel Dorfman, Coco Fusco, Barry Gifford, Martha Long, Luis Negrón, Hwang Sok-yong, Lee Stringer, and Kurt Vonnegut, to name a few, together with political titles by voices of conscience, including Subhankar Banerjee, the Boston Women's Health Collective, Noam Chomsky, Angela Y. Davis, Human Rights Watch, Derrick Jensen, Ralph Nader, Loretta Napoleoni, Gary Null, Greg Palast, Project Censored, Barbara Seaman, Alice Walker, Gary Webb, and Howard Zinn, among many others. Seven Stories Press believes publishers have a special responsibility to defend free speech and human rights, and to celebrate the gifts of the human imagination, wherever we can. In 2012 we launched Triangle Square books for young readers with strong social justice and narrative components, telling personal stories of courage and commitment. For additional information, visit www.sevenstories.com.